'Til the Sun Comes Up

Book Eight, MacLarens of Fire Mountain
Contemporary Western Romance

SHIRLEEN DAVIES

Books Series by Shirleen Davies

<u>Historical Western Romances</u>
Redemption Mountain
MacLarens of Fire Mountain Historical
MacLarens of Boundary Mountain

<u>Romantic Suspense</u>
Eternal Brethren Military Romantic Suspense
Peregrine Bay Romantic Suspense

<u>Contemporary Western Romance</u>
MacLarens of Fire Mountain Contemporary
Macklins of Whiskey Bend

The best way to stay in touch is to subscribe to my newsletter. Go to my Website *www.shirleendavies.com* and fill in your email and name in the Join My Newsletter boxes. That's it!

Description

He's the one who set the rules. Now he wants to change the game.

Skye MacLaren's life revolves around her family and the fierce bucking bull stock they provide to rodeos. She's competitive and competent, having no room in her life for a relationship—including one with a world champion rider and business competitor.

Gage Templeton's rodeo past and executive position with a national bucking stock supplier assures him of exciting work and nights with any woman he chooses. He'll let no one get close—until his company partners with a competitor, forcing him to work with the one woman who could turn his resolve upside down.

Knowing a relationship is the last thing either needs, both charge ahead, certain they can keep their explosive feelings for each other in check—and away from curious family and friends. Continuing their secret encounters becomes even harder when outside forces threaten both their businesses and the people they care about.

As Gage works to discover the threat meant to cripple his company, Skye's doubts increase. She wants more from the most magnetic man she's ever known, but protecting her heart must come first.

Desire, distrust, fear, and the pain of the past cloud their minds, even as they work together to identify the danger. Can two strong, determined people conquer the perils to their lives as well as their hearts?

'Til the Sun Comes Up, book eight in the MacLarens of Fire Mountain Contemporary western romance series, is a full-length novel with an HEA and no cliffhanger.

'Til the Sun Comes Up

Prologue

Houston, Texas

"Hey, man. I appreciate you taking me to the airport." Gage Templeton sipped his beer, glancing down at the burger and fries he'd barely touched.

"Anything for my big brother. Besides, when you included beer and dinner, there wasn't a choice." Brent Templeton popped another fry into his mouth, a cocky grin spreading across his face. "When do we have to leave to catch your flight?"

Gage checked the time. "Fifteen minutes. Then you can get back to the newest woman in your life."

Brent's smile faded for an instant before he covered the slip by taking the last bite of his burger. "You know how it is. We single men have to fill our time somehow."

Gage had become used to his brother razzing him about getting married a few years before. From the beginning, his family made no secret about their dislike for Gwen. Looking at the strained relationship he and his wife shared, Gage had to admit they were right.

When he first met Gwen, she'd been a *buckle bunny*, a woman who chased after professional rodeo riders. Even though he believed she saw him as a trophy, some sort of conquest, something about her had intrigued him. After a few times together, her motives seemed to change.

Looking back, he sometimes wondered why he'd continued seeing her as she followed him from town to town. Even though she was selfish and vain, he'd let her beauty and her superb skills in bed overrule his brain. When it came time to leave the pro circuit, she'd followed him to Houston and his new job at Double Ace Bucking Stock. In time, they married and bought the house she wanted in the *right* section of town, even though it increased his commute and was unlike anything Gage would've chosen for himself.

"You ready, old man?"

Gage glanced up, shaking the memories from his mind, seeing Brent standing next to him, holding out the check. Grabbing it from his brother's hand, he stood. "Yep. Let's get out of here."

******

"Call me when your flight gets in," Brent yelled through the window of his white dually, watching Gage lift his bag out of the truck bed. "Have a safe trip."

Gage nodded as his brother revved the engine and drove away. Probably off to another bar, another woman. He'd long ago given up trying to keep track of Brent's personal life.

Walking through the automatic glass doors, he turned toward the ticket counter of the airline the company always used. Once in a while, he got lucky and took the company plane. Most times, he tried to fit his long legs and wide frame into a too small coach seat.

"Sorry, sir. All flights in and out of Oklahoma City have been cancelled due to the tornado threat. We can try to get you on a flight tomorrow, assuming the warning is removed by then." The young man's face showed the right amount of remorse at the bad news, which didn't help Gage's internal reaction.

"What about another airline?"

The clerk tilted his head and looked at him. "All flights on *all* airlines are cancelled, sir."

"Yeah. Got it. Go ahead and see what you can get me on tomorrow. The earlier the better."

Fifteen minutes later, he walked outside, flagged down a taxi, and headed home. At least he'd be able to spend the evening with Gwen, an occurrence that had become rare between his travel schedule and the appointments filling her days. For a woman who didn't work, she sure could fill her time.

The trip home took longer than normal, giving him time to call the client in Oklahoma to explain and reschedule the meeting. At least his contact was a friend from Gage's rodeo days and an existing Double Ace client.

Climbing out of the cab, his gaze settled on a white dually across the street, recognizing the various stickers on the back window. Turning, he walked to the front door and pulled out his key, taking a quick glance over his shoulder, a stab of warning shooting through him. He couldn't figure out a reason why Brent would be at his house. He and Gwen had never gotten along, stayed as far away from each other as possible whenever he visited.

Shaking off what he considered a misspent sense of dread, he unlocked the door and stepped inside, dropping his bag on the floor. He looked at the large living and dining rooms, not feeling it necessary to announce his presence. Walking into the kitchen, he grabbed a bottle of water, then started up the stairs. Halfway up, he stopped.

He heard the unmistakable sound of Gwen's laughter, followed by a deep drawl he'd recognize anywhere. His heart thudded as the laughing turned to moans, then Gwen's voice as she told the man what she wanted.

The urge to turn and leave, pretend he didn't know what he'd see if he walked into his bedroom, almost won over his need to accept what was happening in his own home. Sucking in a deep breath, he finished climbing the stairs, stopping outside the open door. The sight would've made him gag if the anger he felt hadn't been so fierce.

Folding his arms, planting his feet shoulder width apart, Gage watched as his brother's naked body covered Gwen's, too engrossed in what they were doing to notice him a few feet away. He couldn't take his eyes off them, his rage turning to revulsion as the reality of their betrayal sunk in. Finally, Brent finished, rolled off Gwen, said a few crude words, then sat up, his eyes going wide, jaw slack when he saw who stood before him.

In one quick move, Gage took Brent by the arm, dragged him off the bed, and threw him against the wall. Later, he'd wonder how he had the strength, given his brother's height and build. Anger and adrenaline were powerful tools.

"Get your clothes on and get out."

Standing, Brent held up his hands. "I can explain."

"I'm sure you can, but it won't be to me. Get out, Brent. Don't come back, don't call, and don't show your face around me again."

Brent grabbed his pants, shoving his legs inside, then pulled up the zipper. "What? You're just kicking me out of your life? I'm your brother."

Eyes filled with pain, anger, and a keen sense of betrayal stared back at Brent, the one man he trusted beyond all others. "Not anymore."

Chapter One

MacLaren Bucking Stock
Crooked Tree, Montana
Four years later…

"Skye, do you have the reports ready for the conference call?" Kade MacLaren stood at the door of her office, lifting a brow at the uncharacteristic chaos on her desk.

"Almost." She dashed around her office, shoving papers into a folder, then stopped, her hands on her hips.

"Missing something?"

"The stats on the rodeos we've completed with Double Ace." Searching through stacks of paper, she grabbed one particular piece, holding it in the air. "Found it."

Nodding, his features relaxed. "I'll meet you in my office in five minutes."

Taking a seat behind his desk, Kade reviewed the notes he'd made for the call, thinking over the last few months.

It hadn't been an easy transition for Kade to leave the corporate headquarters in Fire Mountain, Arizona, to take the leadership role in the bucking stock and consumer horse breeding operations in Montana. It wasn't the job making it challenging as much as working with his half-sisters and brothers, people he didn't know existed until three years before.

At first, he hadn't understood the need for the complete company shake-up the three elder MacLaren brothers engineered. Now he did. Heath, Jace, and his father, Rafe, pushed the next generation of MacLarens to succeed, work together in teams throughout the company, using their talents to the fullest—even if the relationships were strained. Or, in his case, almost non-existent.

Skye breezed into his office, blonde hair pulled into a ponytail, a diet soda in one hand. "Ready?" Setting a notebook and folders on the desk, she sat down, taking a long swallow of her drink.

Without replying, Kade pushed several buttons on his desk phone, then sat back.

"Kade?"

He recognized the voice of his uncle, the chairman of MacLaren Enterprises.

"Good morning, Heath. I'm here with Skye. Are you ready for the call?"

"Waiting for one more person, but Rafe and Jace are here. How're you doing, Skye?"

"Great, Heath. We've had an incredible few weeks. I'm looking forward to my trip to Cold Creek to work with Matt and Cassie."

The three men on the other end chuckled. After a stormy reunion and chaotic courtship, Matt Garner and Cassie MacLaren had married a few weeks earlier. They'd returned from their honeymoon to an overloaded schedule, renewed business travel, and long hours preparing quarterly reports.

"Let me know if you're able to get any quality time with Cassie. I haven't seen my daughter since the wedding."

"Want me to see if Cass can make an emergency trip to Fire Mountain, Heath? Although it might be a bit of a stretch to get her to leave her new husband so soon."

"Not necessary. I'll be making a trip to Colorado next week. Ah, here's the man we've been waiting for. Kade and Skye, Gage Templeton from Double Ace is joining us."

Skye felt her body tense, remembering what happened after their dinner meeting in Cold Creek a few months ago. Gage had offered to drive her back to the hotel where they both had rooms. She'd hesitated, knowing being alone with him wasn't smart, then pushed her doubts aside and accepted his offer.

The attraction between them had been palpable since the first time they'd met, yet neither had spoken of it nor considered acting on it. That night had been different. He'd escorted her up the elevator, then down the hall to her room, tension radiating between them with each step. When they reached her room, Gage had hesitated, surprising her with an invitation to dinner the following night. Skye wanted to, wished she could, but had already committed to meeting Cassie and another friend. He'd accepted it graciously, still not moving from the spot by her door.

She'd thought that would be the end of it. Then he'd reached out and skimmed his fingers down her cheek, tucking a strand of hair behind her ear. Instead of stepping away, he'd leaned down, putting his other hand behind her neck, drawing her to him for the most passionate kiss she'd ever had. The thought of refusing never entered her mind. Skye could still remember the immediate and intense flash of heat, the need to get closer. All she wanted was to open her door, pull him inside, and take whatever he offered. After a time, they'd pulled apart, their breathing erratic.

Instead of doing what she wanted, what they both seemed to want, Skye had let common sense rule. Mixing business with pleasure wasn't smart and never ended well. Besides, she'd never been inclined toward one-night stands, and Matt had assured her that was all Gage offered any woman. Walking into her room alone, closing the door behind her, had been harder than she ever expected. Forgetting the kiss had been impossible.

She'd never been kissed with such immediate desire before. Not even by the boy in college she'd planned to marry. It had taken all her willpower to step away, make the decision not to get involved with a man who set all her senses on alert and her body on fire. They'd seen each other once more, at Matt and Cassie's wedding. Skye did everything possible to keep her distance. Then he'd walked up, grabbed her hand, and led her to the dance floor. After their third dance, he bent down to place a warm, passionate kiss on her lips. Then he straightened, giving her a knowing smile before turning to walk away.

Kade's voice pulled her from the memories, forcing her to focus on the business at hand. Reminding herself a kiss was just a kiss, no matter how special it felt, she sat back in her chair, preparing herself to deal with Gage in a professional, detached manner. Thank goodness they were hundreds of miles apart and he couldn't see her reaction to his voice.

"How are you, Gage?" Kade's brow lifted as he shot her a look, then returned his focus to the call.

"Couldn't be better. From the numbers I've seen, the rodeos we partnered on did exceptionally well. What are your thoughts, Skye?"

"Um, yes…we did quite…well. We, um…" She picked up the Double Ace folder, shuffling through the papers to find the chart showing the results.

"Skye, are you still there?" Heath's voice held a hint of concern.

"Yes, I'm here. If this is a good time, I'll review the chart showing the updated numbers."

"Now is perfect."

Clearing her throat, Skye willed herself to stay calm. Gage was no different than any other man—except for one important difference. Given the positive results of the rodeos they'd partnered on, lusting after him would be a huge mistake. He had more contacts in the rodeo business than anyone, except Matt. Double Ace had become a major competitor in a short period of time, a huge force to have on their side. Jeopardizing the partnership with MacLaren Bucking Stock couldn't happen.

Taking her time, she reviewed the numbers and answered questions, staying silent when Gage added his comments. Several minutes later, an agreement had been reached to submit proposals to six more of the largest rodeos. Double Ace would lead on three, MacLaren would submit to the others.

"Excellent work. I know it took everyone at the offices in Crooked Tree and Cold Creek to make this happen. Gage, please let Ivan know how pleased we all are with the results."

"Thanks, Heath. I'll let him know. If there's nothing else, I'll leave you to the rest of your business."

"Already found a hot date for tonight, Gage?" Kade joked, knowing Gage's tendency to find pleasure wherever business took him.

Skye held her breath, waiting for the reply, although she didn't know why it mattered.

"Uh, yeah. Something like that." Gage's voice had lost some of the humor of before.

She knew her reaction made no sense, yet her spirits fell at the thought of him entertaining another woman.

Gage cleared his throat. "Kade, I'll get with you to schedule a time for me to visit you in Montana again."

"Looking forward to it."

A few minutes later, Skye gathered her folders, saying her goodbyes as the call ended.

"Do you want to tell me what that was all about?" Kade leaned back in his chair, clasping his hands behind his head. He waited until Skye turned toward him, doing her best to pretend she had no idea what he meant.

Samantha, Skye's younger sister, poked her head into the office. "Oh, sorry. I saw the phone line go blank and thought you two were finished. You have a visitor, Kade. He says he has an appointment." Sam walked in, handing the card to Kade.

Reading the name, he smiled. "He's right. Let him know I'll be right down." By the time he looked back to where Skye had been standing, she was gone. *More like escaped*, he thought, his mouth turning up at the corners.

Dropping her empty can of soda into the trash, Skye tossed the folders on her desk, then grabbed a bottle of water from the small refrigerator under a counter. Twisting the top off, she gulped it down, finishing half of it before lifting it from her lips.

She'd been a babbling idiot during the call, all due to the effect one man had on her. Pulling off the band holding her ponytail, she ran her fingers through her hair, then shook it out. Skye had conditioned herself long ago to not let a handsome man turn her head or become a resident in her mind. Gage Templeton had been harder to push from her thoughts.

The man would catch the attention of any red-blooded woman, including Skye. If being handsome were all the man had to offer, she'd have booted his image away long ago. This man had much more to offer than being drop-dead gorgeous with a tall, muscled body to match. Gage was smart, funny, hardworking, and according to Matt, honest and loyal to a fault.

None of what Matt or anyone else said mattered. She had no interest in a relationship—not now, not anytime in the foreseeable future. At twenty-eight, she still had much to accomplish in the family business, and a long list of personal goals.

She'd always seen herself as falling in love, marrying, and having children. The timing had to be right, though. In her mind, doing so in her early to mid-thirties would give her time to fulfill her own goals before giving it all up for others.

Skye had watched her father, Rafe, struggle in a marriage where love had died. Her parents had married early. He'd chosen to go into business with two close friends, a decision her mother hated. She'd insisted on children right away, having three born close together—Mitch, Skye, and Sean. The arguments increased, her mother spending more time shopping and with her girlfriends than home with her children. Skye had thought they'd divorce, but Samantha and then Rhett were born a few years later. Although her father never spoke of it, doing his best to give them all a wonderful life, each year brought new lines of worry to his face, and a greater split between her parents. At some point, her mother had turned to another man.

Their troubles hadn't discouraged Skye away from marriage as it had Mitch. Until he met Dana, her older brother had been a confirmed bachelor. He'd been adamant about never going through life the way their father had, with a woman who didn't appreciate what she had and always wanted more. Dana had been Mitch's miracle.

Skye didn't have those same reservations. What she did have was a need to prove herself in the family business, and check off the short list of items on her bucket list. Then, and only then, would she let herself fall in love, allowing her life to be changed by some rugged, all too handsome cowboy.

"What the hell are you doing here, Salgado?" Kade's smile couldn't be broader as he wrapped his best friend in a bear hug. "Man, it's good to see you."

"Same here, brother. It's been way too long." Ernesto "Nesto" Salgado took a step back, his gaze wandering over the man he'd known since they were kids in school, right here in Crooked Tree. "Never thought I'd come back to this place."

Kade's smile dimmed. "Me, either. Guess I figured it was time to get over the anger and man up. Of course, being sent here by the family may have had a little to do with it. Come on upstairs and tell me what brings you this far north."

Kade led the way, taking notice of Skye's closed door. Most days, she preferred to keep it open, drawing a sense of satisfaction from the everyday noises of an office. Something more than an overly hectic schedule bothered her. As he passed her office, he made a mental note to sit down with her, see if he could help with whatever weighed on her mind. He knew there was still a great deal he had to learn about his half-sister.

"In here." Kade gestured for Nesto to precede him. "Water, soda, beer?"

"A bottle of water would be great. Thanks." Nesto walked around the office, noting the pictures. He recognized many from Kade and Brooke's wedding in Fire Mountain. One in particular grabbed his attention. It was of the four of them—Kade, Brooke, Paige, and him—all smiles on a beautiful day.

"That's one of my favorites." Kade stood next to him, clasping a hand on his shoulder. "So, how is Paige?"

"I wouldn't know. She left a few months ago."

Kade's face fell at the dissolution in Nesto's voice. They'd both sworn off long-term relationships years ago when they entered the Army, then transitioned to Special Forces. Years later, Nesto left the service for a job as a U.S. Marshal, while Kade became an undercover agent with the DEA. During all those years, neither had ventured anywhere close to a committed relationship.

Then Kade met Brooke during an investigation, his determination to stay single deteriorating. Nesto hadn't understood Kade's fall until he'd met Brooke's good friend, Paige Wallace. They'd clicked right away and stayed together when the odds were against them. Until she surprised him and walked out.

"Jesus. Why didn't you tell me?"

Nesto shrugged, moving along the wall of photographs. "I kept hoping she'd come back." Turning, he removed the cap on the water bottle and took a long swallow. Swiping a sleeve across his mouth, he glanced up. "A bad habit Paige hated. I guess there was a lot more she hated, but failed to tell me."

"Sounds as if you need something a little stronger than water."

Nesto held up a hand. "Already been that route, man. I found it didn't do any good—made the anger worse rather than burying it." Lowering himself into a chair, he waited until Kade did the same. "I left the marshal service."

Kade stared, his gaze intent, not responding.

Nesto studied the bottle in his hand, as if trying to memorize the label. "It was time. With my military and civilian time added together, I had enough to retire." He chuckled, still not looking up. "Barely." Studying the bottle gave way to picking at the label, peeling it off in frustratingly tiny pieces. "I had some time on my hands, so…"

"Glad this is the spot you chose." Kade checked his watch. "It's time I got out of this place for a while. Sometimes it's more a prison than a place of work." Grabbing his cowboy hat, he signaled for Nesto to follow him downstairs. "Sam, let the others know I'm gone for the day. If I have any appointments, either give them to Skye or cancel them."

Sam started to reply, but Kade waved her off as they headed outside. "We'll take my truck."

They climbed inside, Nesto stroking his hand over the worn leather. "Still have the gray ghost."

Kade chuckled at the nickname they'd given his truck when he drove it off the dealer's lot. Four-wheel drive, raised, with gunmetal gray paint, he'd kept it sticker free, adding no other embellishments.

"I can't imagine life without it."

"Or your chopper?" Nesto asked.

"Damn straight. Still have yours?"

"You couldn't pry that machine from my cold, dead hands. Wherever I settle, she'll come with me. That bike's been my main escape since Paige left."

"Along with the whiskey?" Kade joked.

Nesto snorted. "Between the two, the bike wins, hands down. No hangover and cheaper to operate. At least in the short-term."

Kade pulled onto a gravel road, following it until it ended in a rutted parking lot. A building in dire need of some TLC sat near the back, a sign announcing Dude's Last Chance hanging above the door.

"Dude's? Seriously?" Nesto almost smiled as he opened the door and stepped to the ground.

"On my honor. The guy who built it was named Dude, as in can't sit a horse if he were strapped on. Died in a motorcycle accident a few years ago. Left it to his son." Kade opened the door to a dimly lit bar.

"Let me guess. Also named Dude." Nesto followed him inside, letting his eyes adjust to the darkness.

"Hell no. He goes by DJ. Dude Junior."

"Hey, Kade. Don't usually see you in here this early." A young man with long blond hair secured with a leather thong at the back of his neck stood behind the bar.

"Special visitor. Nesto, this is DJ, best bartender, cook, and waiter on this entire block. DJ, this is U.S. Marshal Ernesto Salgado. We grew up together a few miles from here."

"No kidding. A marshal, huh?" DJ gripped Nesto's extended hand.

Nesto made a show of looking at his watch. "Retired as of four days, twelve hours, and ten minutes ago."

"In that case, a round on the house. What'll you have?"

"At eleven in the morning, it's got to be whiskey." Kade settled onto a barstool.

"Make it two. Same as the good ol' days when we'd return home from deployment." Nesto took the glass DJ handed him. "To old friends and new beginnings." He clinked it with Kade's, then DJ's, downing it in one swallow. "Damn, that's good."

"Only the best for you two." DJ smiled, then slapped the bar. "That's my limit. Let me know if I can whip you up a burger. Kade, you know where to find the drinks." He headed to the back, leaving them alone.

"Nice kid." Nesto leaned his arms on the bar, glancing up at the television on the wall.

"That *kid* served two tours in Afghanistan. He's got the tattoos and scars to prove it."

"Army?"

Kade grinned. "What else? Dude was in the Army, so that's where DJ went. He's trying to keep the place going while he finishes college. From what I can tell, he's got a good head for numbers. I told him to come see me when he graduates."

"MacLaren Enterprises doing that good, huh?" Nesto watched as Kade walked behind the bar, grabbing two mugs. Filling each with a local brew, he handed one to Nesto.

"Better than good." Taking his seat again, Kade turned to his friend, his expression serious. "Now, tell me what happened."

Chapter Two

Double Ace Bucking Stock
Houston, Texas

Gage dashed from his truck to the entrance of Double Ace, trying to stay as dry as possible in the sudden thunderstorm. Juggling a takeout cup of coffee in one hand and his computer case in the other, he used his back to push open the heavy glass door.

"Dang, where did that come from?" The mumbled question wasn't meant for anyone to hear as he stood inside, shaking off the water.

"The sky, my friend."

Gage whipped around to see his boss, Ivan Santiago, a few feet away, a similar takeout cup of coffee in his hand.

"Ivan. I didn't know you were flying in today. I could've picked you up at the airport. Let me put these down."

"No problem, my friend. I needed a car for some meetings later today. I'll walk with you back to your office." Ivan nodded at the receptionist, Daria, who touched a button, allowing passage to offices in the back and upstairs.

"I still don't know why your father and uncles felt the need to put in a state-of-the-art security system." The frustrating extra step to reach his own office still nagged at Gage.

Ivan nodded. "At least they provided a hand sensor."

Gage cocked his head, holding up the cup in one hand and his computer case in the other, illustrating the uselessness of the hand sensor in many cases.

Chuckling, Ivan followed Gage upstairs and into his office. "Their decisions sometimes baffle even me, and I'm family." Ivan's father and two brothers owned the majority share of Double Ace, two other wealthy families from Mexico and two American investors holding the minority. He might be a senior executive in the company, but Ivan oftentimes became aware of major decisions made by his father and uncles at the same time as other employees. It was the main reason for his visit to the Houston office today.

"How is life in El Paso?" Gage set down his coffee and computer case, opening it to get set up, then sat down.

Ivan lowered himself into one of the large leather chairs across from Gage, crossing a leg over his thigh. "As expected. I'm spending more time at the office in León. I find if I'm in Mexico, I'm more able to learn what my family is doing rather than if I wait for a memo."

Gage winced. They'd spoken openly of the communication challenges when Ivan, his father, Javier, and Ivan's aunt, Reyna, had attended Matt and Cassie's wedding a few months before. Javier understood their frustration at having little control over how the business operated, acknowledging his two brothers ruled with iron fists. The good news came when Javier informed them he'd decided to take a more active role in the bull, cattle, and horse stock part of the business. Communication had improved a little. At least until a security company showed up without warning a few weeks before, causing a lot of confusion and discontent among the employees—including Ivan.

"Working with family is never easy. I see it each time I visit the MacLaren offices."

Ivan sat up straighter, setting the coffee aside. "Are there problems I am unaware of?"

Gage held up a hand. "None. In fact, the partnership couldn't have gotten off to a better start. Actually, your timing is perfect. I planned to call you with the information I received while at MacLaren headquarters in Fire Mountain." Pulling the file from his computer case, Gage slid the folder over to Ivan. "Take a look."

Ivan's gaze moved quickly across the columns and down the pages, absorbing the data. "This is quite a remarkable achievement after such a short period of time. I trust you've already begun to negotiate plans for more joint ventures." Ivan's voice, rich and cultured, reflected his Ivy League education, serving as a reminder to Gage how different they were from each other.

"Already started. I should have the agreements by this afternoon."

Ivan closed the folder, setting it on the desk. "Excellent." Picking up his cup, he held it to his lips without drinking, his eyes narrowing. After a moment, as if coming to a decision, he took a large swallow. "I believe we may have a problem, my friend."

This time, it was Gage who straightened, leaned forward, then waited for Ivan to explain.

"What I have to say stays in this room."

"Of course." Gage stood, refilling Ivan's cup, then his own before locking the door to his office and sitting back down.

Standing, Ivan glanced at Gage before walking to the window, peering at the cattle pens below. "My father is concerned about some issues he's seen in the shipments of cattle. To be more specific, he has suspicions about the trucking company my uncles have partnered with to bring the cattle to the U.S."

Gage nodded. He'd wondered why they stopped using their own trucks, but he hadn't questioned it. Once Ivan's uncles made a decision, few bothered to probe deeper.

"Has your father spoken to his brothers about his concerns?"

Ivan turned from the window, leaning his back against the wall, crossing his arms. "No. He came to me first. My father does not want to upset his brothers unless he has more information to support his, shall we say, instincts."

Gage rubbed his chin. He'd always believed in instincts, deferring to his many times when logic went in a different direction.

"He can find no sound financial reason to use an independent trucking company. Unfortunately, he'd been immersed in other family business when the decision was made. Over the last few months, I've urged him to take a more active role in the stock operations." Ivan chuckled, although his face showed no sense of amusement. "A month ago, he walked in on one of his brothers' private meetings, telling them he intended to be more involved."

"I can only imagine their reaction."

"They've always been competitive, each trying to capture the attention of my grandfather. He was a hard man, not tolerant of mistakes, and trusted no one, not even men who'd been his friends since childhood. Understand, Gage, I use the term *friends*, but I'm sure it doesn't mean what you think."

"Enlighten me."

"Grandfather had a small group of men he considered confidantes." Ivan moved back to his chair, lowering himself, then leaning forward. "My family did not always have wealth or status. Those did not come about until my grandfather's time. He built businesses from nothing, using whatever means he deemed necessary to succeed."

"Are you telling me he was a Mexican mobster?" Gabe's smile faded when Ivan nodded.

"The description is accurate. His friends were held to the same standards as any other man. If they went against his orders, failed to do their jobs, they weren't demoted. They disappeared."

Gage's brow lifted. "He thought they knew too much?"

"Precisely. There were no second chances for men close to him. Over time, the sons of some of the *friends* grandfather eliminated began their own businesses." Ivan picked up his coffee, finishing the cooled liquid in a few swallows. "They specialized in *different* products than my grandfather."

"Drugs."

Ivan nodded. "Those organizations became friendly competitors, dividing the territory where they did business. Two, in particular, became quite successful and are still in operation today. They did all they could to run my grandfather and his sons out of business. When my grandfather died, my father and uncles approached these businessmen. They believed burying the past, working together, could reap them all bigger profits."

"Are we talking about the cartels?" Anyone who did business in a border state such as Texas knew about the massive amounts of illegal drugs flowing in from Mexico.

"We are. My father insisted we not form any partnerships with the cartels. Even though they had their differences, my father is the oldest brother. My uncles deferred to his wishes. At least that's what they agreed to do. Now he believes otherwise."

Gage pushed up from his chair and walked to a file cabinet, withdrawing several folders. "These are my records of shipments with the new trucking company. I didn't find anything that concerned me when I reviewed them, and I doubt what we're looking for will be found in any official documents. What does your father want us to do?"

"Keep watch. Look for anything suspicious. I suggest increasing the number of guards we already have posted." Ivan checked his phone, then stood. "I have a meeting downtown, then a dinner meeting before flying back to El Paso tonight."

Gage walked Ivan out, looking around to be sure they weren't overheard. "There are no shipments scheduled until next week. When do you want to talk again?"

"As soon as the shipment leaves Mexico. Use my personal cell number, not the Double Ace one."

"Do you think you're being monitored?" Gage hadn't thought that far ahead, his mind still reeling from the possibility

Double Ace had become entangled in anything to do with the cartels.

"If what my father believes is happening, yes."

Gage followed Ivan outside, then watched as his boss drove away from the stockyard. Thinking over what they discussed, he couldn't help shifting his stance, looking around to see if he were being watched. He didn't spook easily. When he rode professionally, he never allowed himself time to fear an animal or consider the consequences. He focused on what it took to win an event, beat the clock and the beast he rode.

The life he led now couldn't be more different. Meetings, spreadsheets, and contract negotiations were an eternity away from roaring crowds and groups of buckle bunnies.

Gage cringed when he thought of the one rodeo groupie he'd fallen for. The one he should have never let get close. It had been four years since the day he'd walked in on them. Four years since he had any contact with his brother.

Their mother continued to encourage him to forgive Brent and move on. As much as he loved her, this was one thing Gage would never agree to. Friends didn't poach another man's woman. Not ever. The fact it had been his brother, and that he caught them, would always haunt him. He couldn't think of a single circumstance where that would change. The betrayal ran too deep, where forgiveness didn't exist.

At least the image of Brent and Gwen together no longer tore at him during sleep. The divorce had taken two years to finalize. The property settlement almost two years more, which still angered him. She'd contributed nothing, yet he had to sell their home and the one investment property he'd managed to acquire in order to cut her from his life. Not once in all that time had either one of them mentioned Brent.

The worst part was Gwen begging for forgiveness, swearing she'd never meant to hurt him, wanting another chance. The decision to walk away had been an easy one. Gage no longer had to work at seeing her the way his parents had—greedy and self-serving. The woman didn't have the ability for true guilt or shame. His mother believed Gwen had no heart at all. Gage had no problem believing it.

Taking the stairs to his office, his mind drifted to another woman, one who couldn't be more different from his ex-wife. Unlike the cool fascination he'd first had for Gwen, Gage felt an attraction to Skye MacLaren he would never have believed if it didn't hit him each time he saw her. The first sight of her was like nothing he'd ever experienced. Sudden, intense, and overpowering to the point he couldn't be around Skye without wanting her.

The women he spent time with were as different from Skye as sugar is to salt. They were a quick and easy distraction, mindless sex to relieve his stress and fill his time. He rarely saw any of them again, never taking them to bed more than once. Deep inside, Gage knew if he ever let Skye get close, ever made love to her, neither one of them would be the same. It was a chance he wasn't willing to take.

Matt had once caught him staring at Skye, asking why he stayed away. Gage had no answer, except self-preservation and a deep-seated fear of failing again. He'd once believed in marriage being a sacred vow, a promise between two people for life. He no longer gave in to such foolishness. He took whatever women were willing to give, and if they were like Gage, they walked away with their dignity and heart intact.

Settling behind his desk, Gage stared at the mountain of paperwork. He picked up one message, scribbled a note, then set it aside. Moving through the stack, he shook his head, thinking of the repetitiveness of each day.

Each morning, Gage started with an hour run, followed by a shower, then a trip to the local drive-through coffee hut. He'd get to the office by seven, review the day's agenda, make endless rounds of calls, and lock his office when he left around eight that night. The remaining hours would take one of two paths—drive home with a passenger seat full of takeout, or stop at a local tavern, down a few drinks, then perhaps accompany a woman home. He never stayed the night, and never, ever took them to his place. In fact, he rarely asked their name, and if they told him, he didn't pretend to remember.

Gage had no delusions about the decline his personal life had taken. He made no excuses for it, either. What he did have was an excellent job working for a man he respected, a home in a safe, if not opulent, area on the outskirts of Houston, and the freedom to spend his free time as he chose. If he chose to spend his time with beautiful women who offered little but their bodies, he'd accept it without complaint.

Daria's voice came through the intercom. "Gage, you have a call on your line."

His head jerked to the phone on his desk. He'd been so lost in thought, he hadn't even heard it ring. Without asking who it was, he picked it up.

"Gage Templeton."

"It had been so long, I thought perhaps you weren't going to answer."

He tensed, swallowing the immediate lump in his throat at the sound of Skye MacLaren's husky voice. Unlike Gwen, whose voice could grate on a man, Skye's voice drew you in, begging you to lean close so as not to miss a word. Straightening in his chair, he took a breath.

"Miss MacLaren. To what do I owe the pleasure of a call?"

"I had to make a quick trip to Houston to take care of some business for my father. I know it's Friday and you may already have plans, but I thought I'd see if you had time for me to stop by the office."

"I have a better idea. How about dinner?" The instant he spoke, Gage wished he could take the invitation back. He had no business being alone with her.

Her eyes widened. "If you don't have other plans, then yes, as long as it's casual. I didn't bring anything other than jeans and boots."

He could hear the laughter in her voice, picturing her looking down at the clothes she wore.

Gage was glad she couldn't see the smile spreading across his face. "Jeans and boots are perfect. I'll pick you up at seven. Where are you staying?"

She gave him the name and address of her hotel, agreeing to meet him in the lobby, then hung up, leaving him to stare at the phone and wonder what he'd just done. His only excuse was a case of insanity.

Skye tossed her cell phone aside, then fell back on the hotel bed, letting out a relieved breath. The business her father, Rafe, needed done had taken little time, leaving her alone in a big city, her flight out not until the following day. An old college friend lived in a sprawling house on the other side of town. She had three kids and a husband who wrote software programs from home. She could've called her, but when she picked up the phone, her fingers punched in the number to Double Ace.

The butterflies in her stomach had been so thick, she'd been an instant away from hanging up when the receptionist answered. It seemed to take forever for Gage to pick up, and when he did, she felt the familiar pang of fear. The same unnerving panic she had to push down every time she saw him or heard his voice.

During the entire plane ride from Missoula, Skye struggled with what to do. One minute, she pushed all thoughts of Gage aside, focusing on the reason for her trip, deciding to call her girlfriend and invite herself over for dinner. In the next instant, she'd chide herself for being a coward. MacLarens did not shy away from a difficult task or hard work. They faced it head-on and dealt with it. If Gage could be filed under *hard work* or *difficult task*, she'd have no problem taking care of business.

Instead, she found herself in an unexpected and strange situation. One she needed to get control of or walk away. And she never walked away. Well, unless you counted her reaction to her cheating fiancé. She'd thrown a vase and marched from the apartment they'd shared during their final year in college.

Years later, no one had captured her interest. Skye had been with one man—her fiancé. When she'd discovered the truth, she'd backed off, deciding a long break from any kind of relationship suited her just fine. Then Gage Templeton walked into her life.

Using the excuse of him being a client had been a partial truth. Fear of her immediate attraction to him was a more accurate reason she'd pushed him away.

Coming to Houston gave her the perfect opportunity to see if her fascination with him came from a simple case of desire—lust, if she were being honest—or more. Perhaps one dinner would provide few answers, but at least it would give them a chance to talk, learn more about each other, and see if there was anything worth pursuing.

A long distance, casual friendship with benefits might lift her spirits. And as long as Gage wasn't interested in anything permanent, such as marriage, a white picket fence, and children, it might work well for them both.

Chapter Three

Gage sat in his truck outside the hotel, drumming his fingers against the steering wheel. He'd been in the same spot for half an hour, killing time until seven o'clock, when he'd agreed to meet Skye in the hotel lobby.

He'd changed his mind several times since her call. In the end, Gage decided dinner with one of his business partners wasn't unusual, except for the minor detail about his strong attraction to this particular business partner. The answer seemed simple. Stay focused on business, ask about the family members he'd met, and end the evening. Easy.

Walking through the automatic doors, he looked around, sucking in a breath when he spotted Skye stepping out of the elevator. He couldn't remember ever seeing her in such skin tight jeans or snug blouse. Most times, she wore her blonde hair clipped at the back of her neck. Tonight, it hung loose around her shoulders, making her look younger than her late twenties, which he had learned from Matt. When she turned, locking her gaze on his, he felt a punch to his gut as if he'd been kicked by a bronc. If possible, her smile brightened as she walked up to him.

"Hope I didn't keep you waiting. Pop called as I was ready to leave." She held out her hand.

Gripping it, holding it an instant longer than necessary, Gage shook his head. "I just got here. You look, uh…casual."

He grimaced at the lame comment, glad when she began to laugh.

"Hope I didn't dress down too much."

"No, not at all." Forcing his gaze to stay locked on her face and not let it wander down her trim form, he took a step away. "I thought we'd go to this family restaurant with the best steaks in Houston. Or there's a Chinese place—"

Skye held up her hand, a grin tugging at the corners of her mouth. "Steak is perfect." She'd never seen Gage as anything other than in total control, calm to the point of being frustrating.

"Okay then. I'm parked out this way." He walked behind her as they left the hotel and strolled down the block.

Holding the passenger door open, he waited until she climbed inside, then took his time walking around the truck. He didn't know what had come over him. When Skye held out her hand, it took all his willpower to not pull her to him and kiss her the way he wanted. Never had he felt so on edge around a woman.

Scrubbing a hand through this hair, he climbed into the cab and started the engine. "It's not far."

Skye shifted in the seat to face him. "I'm in no hurry. Do you mind taking me for a short tour before we eat?"

Something about the way she said it caught his attention. Turning on the engine, he leaned back, studying her face. Resting his arm across the back of the seat, he couldn't help but think there might be more going on than a pending dinner. "What do you want to see, Skye?"

"Anything. I've only been in Houston a few times and never saw much outside the airport, Double Ace, and my girlfriend's house. The fact is, I've never stayed longer than one night. Not much chance to see the city."

His gaze intensified as he listened. She had this way of looking at him, setting off every warning instinct he had. Even so, all he could think about was reaching across the seat and tugging her onto his lap.

"Gage?" Her smile faded under his intense stare.

"No problem, Skye. We'll take some time to see a few of my favorite places, then eat. Unless there's somewhere specific you want to go."

"Nope. Any place you want to show me would be great. In fact, getting out of the hotel is better than ordering a pizza."

Relaxing, believing he may have misread the direction of their conversation, he pulled into traffic, noting the sun beginning to set. "How do you feel about bats?"

The time flew by. He hadn't been kidding about the bats, taking her to a spot under a bridge. No, she didn't like bats, but anyone would be impressed with the numbers of them swarming around the bridge at sunset.

Next, he took her to a park with a sixty-four-foot wall of water. They enjoyed the sights as he talked about the area, what he did when he had free time. At one point, he grabbed her hand, letting it go an instant later. She wished he hadn't. Her hand in his felt good, right.

The last stop was Discovery Green. Concert music filled the night air as they strolled by a large lake. Stopping by the water's edge, Gage sat down on the grass, then stretched out his legs and lay back, nodding for her to join him.

She sat cross-legged, glad to be wearing jeans. "This is a lovely place, and right in the middle of town."

Placing his hands behind his head, he focused on the night sky. "I heard about this park when I traveled the rodeo circuit. When I moved here to take the Double Ace job, it was one of the first places I visited. Some nights, it's quiet. Others, like tonight, there are people everywhere."

Skye glanced over at Gage, seeing his eyes closed, giving her the perfect opportunity to study his profile. Strong and angular with a straight nose and full lips, she hadn't ever noticed the thin scars at the edge of one eye, probably the result of the bareback or saddle bronc events he excelled at.

"You're staring."

She jerked her gaze away, biting her lower lip. "I have no idea what you're talking about."

His eyes still closed, he chuckled. "I can sense when you're looking at me."

"I thought you'd fallen asleep."

Glancing over at her, he sat up, his serious expression surprising her. "Not much chance of that with you a foot away."

She started to say something, then stopped.

He continued to watch her, seeing her chest move in and out with each breath. Standing, he reached for her hand. "Let's get dinner."

They walked the few blocks to the steakhouse, Gage never dropping her hand. Skye held his as if she had the right, as if they were together, instead of two single people passing the time.

They stopped in front of a building that looked as if it had been there for generations. Stepping inside, a short, rotund woman dashed up, wrapping her arms around Gage.

"It's been too long," she scolded before noticing Skye. "Ah, you brought a lady friend." The woman winked at her, lowering her voice. "He never brings women in here."

Skye felt her face flush at the unexpected announcement, a warm feeling flowing through her.

"Now, Marie. Don't go telling all my secrets. This is Skye MacLaren. We aren't an item. Her company does business with Double Ace."

The warmth Skye felt vanished.

Marie's face fell. "Don't tell me that. I thought you'd finally found a woman to share your life."

Gage looked at Marie, then Skye, but didn't respond.

Skye stepped forward to relieve the awkward silence. "It's nice to meet you, Marie. I'm in town for business, and Gage was kind enough to show me around."

"And bring you to his favorite restaurant." Marie smiled at her.

"Gage Templeton. I wondered why Marie was taking so long out here." A tall, thin man walked up, extending his hand. "It's been too long."

"A couple weeks, Tony."

"And who is this lovely lady?"

Gage turned toward her. "This is Skye MacLaren."

"It's a pleasure to meet you, Tony."

"Ah, pretty *and* friendly." Tony grinned, displaying a gold-rimmed tooth. "Come back this way so we can talk while I cook."

Marie followed right behind him. "He doesn't want to talk to you, Tony. Not when he brought this beautiful woman in for dinner."

"It's all right. Gage and I are on a business dinner." Although the truth, the admission tasted sour in her mouth.

"Still, I will not have you sitting next to the grill. Over here." She took them to a table with a view toward the park a few blocks away. "We've been here for three generations. They wanted to tear down this building, but we fought them…and won." Triumph filled her voice. "What would you like to drink?"

Skye ordered whiskey on the rocks. Gage looked at her, then ordered the same.

"I'll leave you alone to decide what you want tonight." Marie glanced at Gage. "And don't say ribeye. It's time to expand your horizons."

Gage chuckled. "Sorry, Marie. I have a terrible hankering for a ribeye and nothing else will do."

"Hankering?" She laughed as she walked away. "Who says that anymore?"

"I like her. She can dish it right back." Skye grinned, placing the napkin on her lap. "So what do you suggest, besides ribeye?"

"You don't like it?" Gage placed a hand on his chest.

"Love it, but tonight is about trying something new." Heat crept up her cheeks at the look he gave her. "Well, let's see." She picked up the menu, burying her face in it.

"Have you decided?" Marie set down their drinks, then grabbed a pad and pencil.

"Why don't you trade in that old notepad for one of those computer gadgets?"

"You know I'm no good with techy stuff, Gage. Besides, Tony can read my writing just fine."

"If that's the way it's going to be…"

"It is. Now, what do you want?" Her voice was stern, but her eyes soft, crinkling at the corners.

"Skye?" Gage asked, glancing across the table.

"New York, medium. Baked potato with whatever you have to put on it."

Marie nodded. "Good. A woman with an appetite. And you?" She looked at Gage.

"The same, except I'll have the ribeye."

"Of course you will," Marie smirked.

They held their laughter until she disappeared into the back.

"Is she always that way?" Skye asked.

"Since I've known her."

Picking up her drink, she took a sip. "Oh. They use the good stuff."

His eyes glistened as they locked on hers. "Nothing but the best for you, Miss MacLaren."

For two hours and over two more glasses of whiskey each, they talked of nothing and everything. Somehow, they both knew the one taboo subject was previous relationships, his or hers.

Marie stopped by a couple times, picking up on their unspoken need to be alone, even if Gage had said otherwise. Skye enjoyed every minute, not wanting the evening to end, yet accepting it would. She'd be on the plane for Missoula in the morning, the spell created over the last few hours broken.

"Are you ready?" Gage asked as he pocketed his credit card and stood, pulling out her chair.

"Yes…and no. I've had a wonderful time, Gage."

He didn't respond. Instead, he held out his hand, grasping hers and not letting go as they stepped into the semi-humid night.

The street seemed deserted compared to the number of people out before they'd gone inside for dinner. Skye let herself drift through the quiet as they walked to his truck. He hadn't said a word since paying the check, nor had he let go of her hand.

It didn't surprise Skye how much she liked Gage. What shook her was the ease with which they talked, the degree of comfort between them, as if they'd known each other for years.

Glancing up at him as they strode along the sidewalk, Skye realized she hadn't laughed so much in a long time. Not even with Cassie, Dana, and Janie during their girls' nights, which didn't occur nearly enough in her opinion. Of course, part of it had to do with the fact Cassie and Janie worked out of the Cold Creek offices, Dana worked in Fire Mountain, and Skye worked in Crooked Tree. Being in three separate states didn't make getting together easy.

Her other good time seemed to be in Houston. Taking another quick glance at him, she wondered if her feelings about the evening were reciprocated. Gage still hadn't spoken to her since leaving the restaurant. The conclusion she drew wasn't comforting.

Somewhere between the salad and last cup of coffee, she'd found herself accepting there might never be anything between them except friendship. Skye told herself she could live with that, knowing she wasn't ready for more. All too soon, they reached his truck and he opened the door.

Before walking to his side, he let his gaze fasten on hers once more. The heat his scrutiny caused had her shifting in her seat, certain he could hear her heart pounding inside her chest. At one point, she felt certain he'd lean down to kiss her. Instead, he closed the door.

Climbing into the driver's seat, Gage looked straight ahead, not putting on his seat belt or starting the engine. A minute passed, then two. Still, he didn't talk.

Skye began to worry she'd said something to offend him, perhaps jeopardizing the relationship between the two companies. She couldn't stay silent when filled with such unease. Ignoring a ball of dread forming deep in her stomach, she unclasped her seat belt and turned toward him.

"Is something wrong, Gage?"

Instead of answering, his heated gaze met hers, studying, searching. For what, Skye didn't know.

In the next instant, he reached over, grabbed her around the waist, and hauled her onto his lap. He didn't hesitate, capturing her mouth in a kiss to match the only other one he'd given her. Merciless, unyielding, and all-encompassing, the kiss went on and on, not letting up until the need for air had them pulling apart, gasping for breath. He rested his forehead against hers, his arm still holding her close.

"I've wanted to do that all night." His rough voice rippled through her.

"So have I." Skye hadn't been able to get their first kiss out of her mind, wishing for one more chance to see if he tasted as good as she remembered.

He pulled back a little. "That a fact?" His eyes crinkled at the corners, his voice full of amusement.

She didn't respond with words. Instead, she wrapped a hand around his neck and leaned down, recapturing his lips. A wave of intense pleasure flashed through her as the hunger between them increased. She could feel his hands move over her back and hips, settling on her waist, tugging her close. His tongue traced the fullness of her lips before delving inside, tasting her, setting her aflame.

Raising his head, he shifted her on his lap, kissing the hollow at the base of her throat, searing a path along her shoulder before brushing his lips against hers once again. Releasing his hold, he brought his hands up to cup her face.

"I should take you back to your hotel."

Licking her lips, tasting him there, she nodded. As she slid off his lap, he put an arm around her shoulders.

"Where are you going?" His smile warmed her. "I want you right here beside me."

Something about his words, the undisguised need in his voice, tore through her. She felt the same need, the same desire to be close. They stayed silent on the drive to the hotel, Gage keeping his arm around her.

After leaving the truck with an attendant, he settled an arm around her shoulders as they stepped into the elevator. She found herself wondering if she should invite him into her room or wait until he asked.

Reaching her floor, they stepped into the hall.

"Which way?"

Skye nodded down the hall. Taking the key card from her hand, he swiped it and pushed the door open, ushering her in before closing it firmly behind them. He tossed his hat on the bed, then settled her against the wall. Taking her face between his hands, his mouth covered hers in a kiss so full of hunger, she moaned against his lips.

Wrapping her arms around his neck, she drew him down, her mind reeling at the heated intensity. Pleasure radiated through her, a desire unlike anything she'd ever felt growing stronger as his body aligned with hers. She wanted more. She wanted everything this man was willing to give, and she didn't want to wait any longer.

When he broke the kiss and stepped away, Skye swallowed hard. "Gage…" She didn't know if it were a plea or a question.

Sucking in a ragged breath, Gage ran a hand through his hair. "Good Lord," he breathed out, finally meeting her gaze. "You have no idea what I want to do to you."

A nervous laugh escaped as she stared up at him, wondering why he'd stepped away. "I have a pretty good idea. It's probably the same as what I want to do to you."

He paced away, then turned to face her, his eyes narrowing. "This isn't a smart idea."

She nodded. "Probably not." If her stomach didn't feel tied in knots, her heart beating wildly, she might have thought it funny he was the one pulling away this time.

"We have to work together."

"I know, Gage." She kept her distance, letting him get out what he needed.

"Matt is a friend."

"Yes. He's said the same of you."

"But he's also part of your family. A family I respect a great deal." His voice began to calm, although he continued to keep his distance.

She took a few tentative steps toward him, not getting close enough to touch. "What do you want?"

"Hell, Skye. I think it's obvious I want you."

Sucking in a breath, she placed a hand on his arm. "I want you, too."

He choked out a laugh. "Here's the thing. I don't want just one night. I'm pretty certain once with you won't be enough."

She started to speak, but he placed a finger against her lips.

"If we *do* decide to go through with this, I need to be clear. I'm not looking for a relationship. I've been down that road once and don't intend to ever travel it again. Fact is, I haven't been with a woman more than once in years. Don't even know the names of most of them. If that makes me sound like a jerk, I guess that's what I am. But with you…"

Her chest squeezed as she waited for him to continue.

Reaching out, he took her hand. "You have to be certain you can accept me on my terms."

Skye bit her lip, willing herself to stay calm. "Then I suppose you should be clear as to what they are."

Dropping her hand, he sat down on the bed, patting the spot beside him.

"I'd rather stand." Skye clasped her hands in front of her.

He leaned forward, resting his arms on his thighs, catching her gaze with his. "All right. We see each other when we can, when it's convenient. No expectations, no late night calls, no drama. I'm free to see other women, and you're free to see other men."

"No."

He straightened. "No? If that's your answer, I'll walk out now."

Turning away, she worked to compose herself. She didn't know why she even considered his demands, except for one thing. She felt the same about all of it, other than one point.

"I'm good with it all…" She hesitated.

"Except?"

"You don't see other women, and I don't see other men. It's non-negotiable for me, Gage. I'm not looking for a relationship, either, but I'm also not looking to feel cheap or used."

Gage stood, holding a hand toward her. "Skye—"

"Please, let me finish." She turned away, gathering her thoughts. "I can live with seeing each other when it works for both of us. No drama, no commitment. Easy and infrequent." She whipped back around, pinning him with a hard stare. "If you need to be with other women, I'm not the person for this kind of *arrangement*."

He winced at the description and the terse tone. "What happens if one of us wants to start seeing someone else?"

"A simple phone call should work." Her voice remained steady. She didn't know why it hurt to say it out loud.

Gage walked up to her and placed his hands on her shoulders, his voice low and rough. "The last thing I want is to hurt you. You have to know I'm not a good bet. This could last a few nights or much longer. Either way, I don't want anything permanent, and I want to walk away as friends."

"I'm a big girl, Gage. I don't want or need anything more than seeing each other whenever we have time. Is that fair?"

His nostrils flared. Studying her face, he saw no sign she didn't believe her own words. Dropping his hands from her shoulders, he picked up his hat, settling it on his head.

Her brows drew together. "Are you leaving?"

"It's best. You need to be sure it's what you want. Truthfully, so do I."

She didn't like it, but knew he was right. "I leave tomorrow."

"Change your flight to Sunday." He smiled. "Please. I'd like to see you tomorrow, show you more of the city, take you downtown for dinner." Stepping closer, he cupped her face in his hands, the kiss slow and warm. Groaning, he stepped away. "Change your flight, Skye."

Chapter Four

Skye couldn't seem to move as he closed the door behind him. He'd asked for exactly what she wanted—friends with no strings, some good times, no expectations. When it ended, they'd walk away with their hearts intact.

Falling back on the bed, she placed an arm over her eyes and groaned. If it were what she wanted, why did she feel so miserable? Neither of them had the time or inclination for a relationship. Work took up most of her time, and what she had left was most often spent with her family. Still, Skye found herself lying awake at night, lonely, wanting more, but not willing to commit the time a relationship required.

She'd never been one for hooking up, and suspected Gage might be tired of spending his free time with women he cared nothing about. This way, at least they'd be with someone they respected, liked, and could find pleasure in. Someone who would ask nothing beyond friendship and nights of passion.

He'd been right to bring it up, make them both face the reality of what they wanted. It didn't mean she liked it, but if they couldn't be truthful with each other, they might as well walk away now and spare themselves the pain.

Sitting up, she rubbed her palms into her eyes, trying to stall the headache threatening. Glancing at the clock, she decided to wait until morning to call the airline and change her flight. No need to go through it all now with her mind fogged from the discussion with Gage.

Stripping off her jeans and blouse, she walked into the bathroom and picked up her brush. Her nighttime routine had always given her a sense of comfort, a familiar end to what had become hectic days. Tonight, she felt agitated, not quite herself. Sighing, she tossed the brush aside.

She needed sleep and time to think. As much as Gage's proposal made sense, it also triggered memories of her past failure. It had taken a long time to get over walking into her apartment to find her fiancé in bed with another coed. To say her confidence took a major blow didn't come close to defining the lack of self-esteem she carried around for months afterward.

This wasn't about possible betrayal, though. It was about two consenting adults sharing their time without expectations of it developing into something more.

Burying herself under the covers, her mind continued to go over the pros and cons of seeing Gage. She thought of her cousin, Cassie, and sister-in-law, Dana. What would she tell them, or anyone else, about the arrangement? The best action would be to do what her brother, Mitch, did with Dana. They kept their relationship a secret for months.

Sighing, Skye closed her eyes. The answers would come…just not tonight.

The ringing of the phone by her bed woke Skye. Pushing back the covers, she grabbed it, putting it to her ear.

"Hello."

"Skye, it's Mitch. There's been an accident."

"Who?" She jumped out of bed, her heart racing.

"Samantha. She was exercising her new horse, making jumps, and…" His voice cracked.

"Skye, it's Dana. Mitch handed me the phone. Sam's in surgery. They haven't told us anything."

"Where is she?" Holding the phone to her ear, she scrambled to dress.

"The hospital in Crooked Tree. How soon can you get here?"

"I'll check out of the hotel in a few minutes. I'll get there as soon as I can."

"Text me with your flight information. I'll send someone to pick you up."

"Thanks, Dana."

Jamming the few clothes she brought into her bag, Skye took one more look around before heading to the elevator. Checking out took a few minutes. Waiting for a taxi took forever. The entire time, she thought of her younger sister and how much she loved to ride. At twenty-two, Sam had everything going for her.

"This can't be happening," she mumbled to herself as the miles passed on the way to the airport.

"Ma'am?" The driver looked at her in the rearview mirror.

"Nothing. Thinking out loud." She drew in a heavy breath. Her father would already be there, as would her brothers, Sean and Rhett. Sam and Rhett were almost four years apart, the youngest of Rafe's children, but they were close.

Her phone vibrated in her purse. Digging through it, she saw Kade's name on the screen.

"Is there news?"

"She's out of surgery." Kade was the oldest of her siblings, as well as her boss. His life hadn't been easy, yet he always seemed in control, able to handle any crisis. "They have her in ICU, but are being vague about what's going on."

"Can you tell me what happened?"

"Her horse missed a jump and stumbled, throwing Sam over his neck. Thank God Rhett was with her. He called 911 right away."

"I'm at the airport. I'll text you and Dana my flight information."

"Do that. And, Skye?"

"Yes."

"Be safe. We don't need anyone else getting hurt racing to the hospital."

She snorted. "You know me, Kade. I'm the safest one in the family."

Hanging up, her thoughts drifted to Gage. As soon as she changed her flight, she'd call him, explain what happened. She had no idea when they'd see each other again. Maybe last night was the beginning and the end, but Skye couldn't focus on Gage right now. Her thoughts and energy had to be on Sam, not on a man who might be nothing more than a temporary distraction.

"I'm sorry, sir. Miss MacLaren checked out early this morning."

"I see. Well, thank you." Gage's spirits fell. He had gotten little sleep after driving home, his mind wrapped around what he and Skye had discussed. Waking early, he'd gone for a run, checked his messages, then finished some paperwork. By eight o'clock, he'd called her cell, sending a text when she didn't answer.

His phone rang as he walked to his truck. Without checking, he put it to his ear. "Gage Templeton."

"Gage, it's Skye."

"Got cold feet, huh?" He tried to sound unaffected by her taking off without a word, sensing he'd failed.

"I'm sorry. Mitch called early. There was an accident."

Gage stopped walking. "Tell me."

"It's Samantha, my younger sister."

"I've met her."

Skye explained, her voice breaking as she spoke. "I planned to call you as soon as I reached the airport, but a seat became available on a flight ready to leave. I took it. I'm in Crooked Tree now. I'm sorry. It must seem as if I ran out on you."

"Skye, listen to me. You did what you had to. I'd offer to fly up, but I know you're surrounded by family. Don't worry about me. Be with Sam. She's the one who needs you."

"Right. Well, my ride just showed up. I'll, um…I guess we'll talk sometime."

"Whenever you want. You know how to reach me." Gage wanted to say more, but held himself in check. He didn't need to make it sound as if he already missed her, wished she would ask him to fly up for support. "I'll let you go."

"Okay then. Goodbye, Gage."

She ended the call before he had a chance to respond. He couldn't believe how much he'd looked forward to spending the day with Skye, showing her the sights, getting to know her better. As he climbed into his truck, Gage told himself her leaving was for the best. Neither one of them needed the complication of getting too close to someone. At least he didn't.

Starting the engine, he thought of Samantha's brilliant smile and boundless energy. He'd met her a couple times, impressed with her wit and attitude. The same as he'd been impressed with her sister. Shaking his head, he hoped it would turn out all right for the young woman.

Somehow, he already felt a loss. He doubted it would go any further with Skye. This had proved to be a sanity check for both of them, something they needed after what almost happened between them the night before. Gage had his work, and Skye had her family. Why would either want to complicate it with the absurd proposal he'd made?

Taking the highway to Double Ace, he reconciled himself to another Saturday at the office. Perhaps another night at one of the many bars, eating alone, wishing a certain blonde were sitting next to him.

Skye ran through the hospital lobby, ignoring the offer of help from the volunteer at the front desk. Thanks to a text from Kade, she knew where to go. Pushing open the door to the family waiting area, she spotted her father and ran into his arms.

"How is she?"

Rafe kissed the top of her head. "She's in recovery. Other than the fact she has a broken arm, bruised ribs, and a concussion, we won't know much else for a few days."

Swiping at tears pooling in her eyes, she pulled away, noticing the others in the room.

"None of that, Skye." Mitch draped an arm around her shoulders, tugging her close. "She's doing well, better than we first thought."

She moved from Mitch's embrace to Sean's. He'd taken over their consumer experience group, better known as the *dude ranch*, a few months earlier. At first, he'd been irritated at being shunted off to a place apart from the rest of the family. Now, he seemed to embrace the autonomy, as well as the attention from the numerous female clients.

"She's going to be fine, Skye." Sean held her in a soothing hug. They were a year apart in age. Growing up, Skye had always wished her younger brother would stop following her around, messing up her life. Now, she felt grateful for the strong arms and whispered words of encouragement.

"Skye?"

She turned in Sean's arms to see Dana a foot away. Hugging her sister-in-law, Skye took her hand, finding chairs next to each other.

"Did anyone call Mother?" Skye glanced around, not wanting anyone to overhear. Her mother wasn't a popular subject in the family.

Dana snorted her disgust. "Sean called her right after he learned about it and offered to arrange a flight out. She declined. Her vacation to Hawaii took precedence. She did ask for Sean to call her with any news."

"I doubt he will." She looked up to see Sean talking with Mitch, Rhett, and their father. "Whenever any of us reach out to her, she shoots us down. There is always something else pressing she has to attend to. I haven't seen her in years."

"You know my feelings about your mother." Dana had never met the woman. She'd sent her and Mitch a note congratulating them on their marriage, and that had been the last they'd heard from her.

Skye's eyes brightened. "We all know how you feel, and we all agree with you." Sitting back in the chair, she looked around, seeing Kade off in the corner, alone. "Brooke still in Fire Mountain?"

Brooke Sinclair MacLaren worked for the company, helping sort out organizational issues between the different entities, transitioning new businesses into the fold. Her Ph.D. could've been used by numerous companies in the country, but she'd chosen to stay with the family.

"Brooke, Annie, and Heath are flying in this afternoon. Rafe told them it wasn't necessary, but you know how they are."

Heath had married Annie Sinclair several years before, welcoming her three adult children, Cam, Eric, and Brooke, into the MacLaren clan. All held positions within the company.

"Jace is staying behind. Lots going on with them, but I'll have to fill you in later." Dana stood when her husband, Mitch, walked over, settling an arm around her shoulders.

"Rafe and Kade are going to stay here. The rest of us are going to the cafeteria for lunch. They'll call when the doctor comes back out."

"I'm not hungry. I'll stay here with Pop and Kade."

"How about we bring you something back, Skye?"

"A soda would be great, Dana. Thanks."

Pulling her phone from her purse, Skye sent a quick message to Gage, letting him know she'd made it to the hospital and what they knew of Sam's injuries. By the time the others returned with her soda an hour later, she still hadn't gotten a response.

"Hey, man. Tell me what I can do to help out." Nesto sat across the cafeteria table from Kade, both ignoring the cups of coffee in front of them.

Kade rested his arms on the table, his shoulders slumped in exhaustion. He and the family had been at the hospital for over twenty-four hours, waiting for more word on Sam. All they'd been told was she was still in ICU and unable to have visitors. More than once, they had to hold Rafe back from storming through the doors to see his daughter.

"I appreciate it, Nesto, but there's nothing you can do. I'm going to stay here a couple more hours, then go to the office. Cassie and Matt are flying up this afternoon to help out."

"It's tough. The waiting, I mean."

"Nothing's worse. The doctor said he'd give us an update soon. When he does, I'm out of here." Kade picked up the coffee and took a sip, grimacing at the taste. "I hate hospitals."

"Yeah, I remember," Nesto snorted. "Ever since you crashed your bike playing chicken with that motorcycle gang."

"Stupid move." It had been almost three years and Kade still suffered from headaches and random pain in his legs.

"But effective. I wouldn't recommend it a second time."

"I do have some news for you." Kade looked up, his mouth curving into a smile.

Nesto's face sobered. "Do *not* tell me you tried to find Paige. If so, I'm out of here right now."

"Nope. This has nothing to do with Paige. It's about a job."

Nesto shook his head. "Come on, man. You know I just retired. It's about kicking back, figuring out who I am, what I want to do."

"You'd be in charge of security for MacLaren Enterprises. Some travel, great pay and benefits, hire your own people, report directly to Cam Sinclair."

"Brooke's brother?"

"That's the one. Don't worry about it, Nesto. I'll tell Heath you aren't interested."

"Hold up, amigo. I didn't say I wasn't interested."

"Good, because you're meeting with him this afternoon. He and Annie flew in late yesterday afternoon. They're staying at Rafe's old house. You'll be meeting him there about three o'clock."

"Geez, man. That doesn't give me much time to get ready." Nesto downed the rest of his coffee, shifting in his seat.

Kade chuckled at his friend's unease. They'd been through numerous missions in their Special Forces days, and Nesto had handled some of the worst criminals as a U.S. Marshal. An interview shouldn't be a big deal.

"Relax. He already knows you. He just wants to go over details, make sure you're ready for a new job and okay with living in Fire Mountain."

"He's your family, bro. I don't want to screw this up."

"If you're not up for it…"

"Screw you. I'm up for whatever. Give me the address." Nesto pulled out a pen and grabbed a napkin, scribbling down directions. "Three o'clock?" Standing, he slid the information in his pocket.

"Yeah. Try to be presentable." He winced when Nesto punched his arm.

Walking out, Nesto turned, pointing a finger at him. "Dinner tonight. You and Brooke. My treat."

Kade felt a sense of peace as Nesto headed out the door. At least something good had happened in the last twenty-four hours. He'd soon have his closest friend working for the family, watching their backs, making sure the company and its people were secure. He couldn't think of a better man for the job.

Chapter Five

Houston, Texas

"Good morning, boss."

Gage finished reading the email he'd received from Kade MacLaren asking to postpone a meeting in Cold Creek, Colorado, for a week. He had no problem with the request. The longer he went without seeing Skye, the easier it would be to ignore his natural response to her.

Eddie "Gonzo" Gonzalez, the stock manager for Double Ace, stood in the doorway, fingering the hat in his hands.

"Sit down, Gonzo. I'm guessing you're here to talk about the additional men we need to hire."

"I've found four men who can start right away. All are ex-military or law enforcement. Do you want to meet them before we make an offer?"

Gage shook his head. "Not necessary. I trust your judgment. What about the other issue? Did you find anything?"

"Nothing. One other employee helped me search the company trucks. We checked everywhere and found nothing."

"You trust this other employee?" Gage knew he didn't need to ask. He'd mentioned the need for complete discretion to Gonzo more than once.

"I do." A sly grin appeared. "He's my nephew, Paco."

"I've met Paco. Is he still in college?"

"He's a senior this year." Gonzo's grin expanded to a proud smile. "Paco will be the first from our family to graduate from college."

"Have him come see me when he does."

"Thank you, boss. I'll tell him. You may not know, but his father, my brother, is a retired Border Patrol agent. He told us what to look for and the places smugglers use to hide drugs. Everything was clean. We could use a sniffer dog."

Gage hadn't told Gonzo about his friend, Thad Montgomery, a former DEA agent who owned a private firm specializing in helping companies legally do business in Mexico. He had access to dogs trained to detect substances such as illegal drugs, explosives, currency, or blood.

"I may be able to help with that. Let me make a call. What about other company trucks, the ones employees drive?"

"There are only three, boss. You, me, and one set aside for Mr. Santiago, although he never uses it. The man prefers to rent a car when he comes to Houston."

Gage chuckled. "I can understand. A few months ago, I rented a sports car in Cold Creek for the MacLaren meetings. It felt nice to drive something fast and sleek."

"I'll have to try it sometime. As far as the three trucks, I'll ask Paco to search them this afternoon, unless you need yours."

"Search mine first. I have a meeting across town later today."

Gonzo nodded. "I sure hope we don't find anything. We could also search the buildings, storage sheds, and trailers."

"No. If an illegal item is brought here, I guarantee it's gone within a few hours. This wouldn't be considered the final destination. If we find something, it will be in the vehicles transporting animals to Houston."

"Unlike our company trucks, the new company unloads the cattle, then leaves." Gonzo glanced at Gage, seeing his eyes narrow, giving him an idea. "We should follow them. Their trucks are never searched by us since they're independent. They may be unloading cattle, then taking other merchandise to a different location."

"I agree, but it's not our job to follow them. At least not yet." Gage hoped there didn't come a time when he or Ivan thought it necessary to do more than keep Double Ace property and operations clean. "Of course, there's no reason we can't have a detection dog onsite the next time there's a shipment."

A slow grin spread across Gonzo's face.

"Do whatever you need to about the three company pickups and let me know if you find anything. I'll let you know if I come up with a detection dog and handler." Gage knew enough to understand not just anyone could work with one of the highly skilled animals. If Thad agreed to help, Gage knew he'd owe his friend big time.

He waited until Gonzo left before reading the email from Kade again. Gage composed a reply, letting him know rescheduling wasn't an issue. He also asked Kade to give Samantha his best.

He'd yet to reply to Skye's text. Reading the message again, he pictured her sitting in the hospital, worried about her sister. Gage had never been good at offering comfort or knowing what to say in this kind of situation. In his family, sympathy over injuries didn't happen. His father believed in tough love. He might push or shove Gage to get his attention. You were expected to stand up and get over it.

The rodeo circuit hadn't been much different. Broken arms, legs, and concussions were all expected. The rodeo doc would patch you up and tell you to take it easy, knowing the instructions would be ignored. Nothing much was said from the guys he competed against.

Rubbing the back of his neck, he tried to think of something to say, a few words to let her know he'd been thinking of Sam and hoping she'd pull through with little damage. He knew quite a bit about her injuries from an earlier text from Kade. He'd responded to that one. Why did he find it so hard to tap out a reply to Skye?

Setting his phone aside, he decided to let it go. In another week, maybe two, he'd see her in Cold Creek for what Kade called a team meeting.

Although he understood the reasons, there were times, like now, he wished his closest friend, Matt Garner, hadn't left Double Ace for the opportunity with the MacLarens. They'd become close, at least as close as Gage would allow himself to get with another man. When he worked with Matt, he knew at least one person at the table understood the workings at Double Ace, the complexities of getting approval from the Santiago family. It was worth the hassles and extra steps to pick up several more large rodeos. And it gave him a chance to be close to Skye.

Gage had made up his mind he wouldn't bring up what they discussed at the hotel. If she brought it up, that would be fine, but he doubted she would. Even if she said otherwise,

Skye wasn't the kind of woman who'd be comfortable with the no strings relationship he required. And he'd always be concerned about hurting her. She deserved more—a lot more than a man with his history could ever offer.

Crooked Tree

"Pop is heading back to Fire Mountain tomorrow, so you'll be stuck with Rhett and me." Skye sat in the hospital room with Sam a week later, checking her email as they waited for the doctor to approve her release. "Kade said don't even think about working. If you do, he'll close down your email and revoke your access to the office."

"Ah, come on, Skye. You've *got* to talk to him for me. I'll go crazy at the house by myself all day. Having another older brother is the worst. Mitch is bad enough. Now there's Kade."

"Who loves you and wants you healed before going back to work. Pop agreed with him."

"He would," Sam groaned, fidgeting with the cast on her left arm. "You know, there's a way to route incoming calls home, then I can reroute them to the right person at the office."

"Save your breath. Kade isn't going to budge. In that regard, he, Mitch, and Pop are exactly alike."

Sam opened the bag Skye had brought containing clothes to change into once the doctor left. "My phone isn't here."

"It's charging at the house. I found it in your Jeep with a dead battery."

"At least my big sister loves me."

Skye placed an arm around Sam's shoulders, surprised at the down mood. Sam always wore a smile, slept little, and jumped out of bed before dawn. She drove the rest of them crazy with her boundless energy.

"It's going to be all right, sweetie. The arm will take a few weeks to heal. If you do everything the doctor says, Kade will let you come back to work in a couple weeks, as long as you don't get on his case about it."

Sam sighed, resting her head on Skye's shoulder.

"Hey."

Sam sat up, her eyes widening. "Tucker? How did you find me?"

"I called your office and begged."

For the first time since the accident, Sam laughed, then put her right arm around her chest. "Please. Don't make me laugh."

"Sorry, baby."

Skye stood, glancing at Sam, than back at Tucker, before clearing her throat.

"Oh. Sorry, Skye. This is Tucker Kimball. He's a friend of mine from college. Tuck, this is my sister, Skye."

"Ma'am."

"Ugh. That makes me sound old. Please, call me Skye." She leaned against the bed, not ready to leave the two of them alone. "You two know each other from school?"

"Yes, ma'…I mean, Skye. We were both on the rodeo team."

"Tuck competed in saddle bronc and bareback events. He got his MBA the same time I got my bachelor's." Sam shifted on the bed, adjusting the uncomfortable hospital gown. "I wonder how much longer until the doctor arrives."

The mention of saddle bronc and bareback riding reminded Skye of Gage and the events he dominated in the pro circuit for a couple seasons before retiring. She sighed, wondering what he was doing, if he were with someone, if she ever crossed his mind. Pushing the thoughts aside, she refocused on the two people in the room.

"Patience has never been Sam's strength, Tucker."

"Don't I know it." Tucker placed his hand on a chair, taking a spot at the end of the bed.

"Hey," Sam protested.

"Tell me it isn't true," Tucker countered. "Doesn't matter if she's waiting her turn for an event, waiting for food, or pumping gas. Nothing ever goes fast enough for her."

Skye laughed. "You obviously know her pretty well."

"Friends, Skye. Tucker and I are just friends." Sam fell back against the pillows, an exasperated expression on her face. "Oh. I forgot to ask about Ernesto."

"Who?" Tucker asked, his brows drawing together.

"This very hot U.S. Marshal who's my brother's best friend." Sam's eyes brightened. "Actually, Kade said he retired and Uncle Heath offered him a job." She looked at Skye. "Tell me it's true."

"It's true, Sam. He's the new head of security. Kade says he reports to work in a few days, after he's settled into a place in Fire Mountain."

"Maybe I can get Pop to let me move to Fire Mountain. There must be *something* I can do down there."

Skye cast a quick look at Tucker. The jovial mood of a few minutes before had been replaced with an expression she couldn't quite define. She wondered if perhaps he had deeper feelings for Sam.

"Sam, Nesto is ten years older than you. And, don't forget, he has a girlfriend, who happens to be Brooke's best friend."

"If he's still with Paige, why is he up here without her?" Sam pursed her lips, her eyes scrunching. "Maybe they've split up."

The doctor strolled in, barely sparing a glance at Skye and Tucker. "I understand you're anxious to leave our fine facility, Miss MacLaren." He looked over Sam's chart. "How do you feel? Anymore headaches?"

"I feel great. No headaches. Other than my broken arm, my ribs hurt when I cough or laugh."

"That's to be expected. Let me go over what you can and cannot do, as well as review the medications you'll be taking home."

An hour later, a hospital volunteer rolled Sam's wheelchair out to Skye's waiting truck.

"Did Tuck leave?" Sam's voice held a tinge of disappointment.

"He'll meet us at the house. I invited him to stay for lunch." Skye opened the passenger door, helping Sam to get settled, then walked around to climb into the driver's seat. "Tucker seems like a real good guy."

"The best. At first, I thought maybe he and I…" Her voice trailed off before she caught herself and plastered a smile on her face. "Turned out he had a steady girlfriend. A few weeks after they broke up, he started dating a friend of mine. It didn't last long. Afterward, I thought maybe he'd take an interest in me, but…" She shrugged. "I realized he'd never see me as more than a friend."

Skye didn't comment about the way Tucker looked when Sam mentioned Nesto. The expression on his face wasn't one of a man unaffected by Sam's musings about Kade's friend.

"You're sure about that?" Skye asked, keeping her gaze fixed on the road ahead.

"Absolutely. The last I heard, he took a job in Seattle. He's probably dating one of those city girls by now. I'm surprised he's out this way."

"Guess you'll have plenty of time to catch up. He's going to stay at the house a couple nights."

Sam twisted toward Skye, grimacing at the pain in her chest. "Geez, that hurts." She wrapped her good arm around her waist and drew in a slow breath. "Why would he stay with us? There must be a reason he's in town, which means he must know somebody."

Skye bit her bottom lip, thinking it was Sam he knew, and she was the reason he'd come to Crooked Tree. They pulled into the driveway, spotting Tucker leaning against his pickup.

"Wow. He got a new truck. The one he had in college was at least twenty years old, all beat up with rust spots. Tuck must be doing well in Seattle."

Skye watched Tucker walk over to Sam's side of the truck. "Let's get you inside, then you can ask him all your questions while I fix us something for lunch."

Sam opened her mouth to reply, then shut it when Tucker pulled her door open.

"You've got two choices. Let me carry you inside or walk. Which will it be?"

"I can walk just fine, Tuck. At least I can if you get out of my way."

He snorted, stepping aside, holding the door wide. "Well, come on. I'm hungry, and Skye said she'd make us lunch."

"Good idea." Skye stood next to Tucker, watching Sam try to navigate off the seat and onto the ground. "Guess I'll leave you two to get into the house while I see what I can pull together."

"Skye, wait." Sam sat perched on the edge of the seat, an odd look of uncertainty on her face as she watched her sister walk away.

Skye held up her hand, not turning around. "You and Tuck figure it out. Meet me in the kitchen when you're ready."

Sam wanted to slap the smirk off Tucker's face. "I just need help getting down, then I can walk by myself."

"That's more like it, Sammy."

"Don't call me that."

He chuckled, sliding a hand behind her back. Instead of helping her to the ground, he slipped his other arm under her legs and gently lifted.

"Tucker." Her protest didn't seem too convincing as she wrapped her good arm around his neck and held on.

"That's better. You just relax. We'll be in the house before you know it." A smile curved the corners of his mouth when he heard her sigh.

Pushing the door open with his boot, he took a quick look around, deciding the sofa in front of the big river rock fireplace would be perfect. Setting her down, he slid his hands away, being as gentle as possible.

"There you go, princess."

She snorted out a laugh. "That's not much better than Sammy."

"You two stay right where you are," Skye called from the kitchen. "I'm fixing sandwiches. I'll bring them in there."

"Do you need a pillow?" Tucker looked down at her, not a trace of the sometimes arrogant cowboy on his face.

"No, this is good. Thanks for helping me."

"Anytime, Sam." Tucker slid his hands in his pockets, then glanced around the massive great room. "This is quite a place." He walked over to a bookcase, sliding a hand along the wood. "This is beautiful."

"My brother, Mitch, made it. He made much of the furniture in the house. Most of what he makes now goes into the house he has with his wife, Dana. At least it did until the uncles moved him down to Fire Mountain. They rent a place now."

Sam closed her eyes, realizing she was rambling. "Sorry. I get carried away sometimes."

Tucker shook his head, ignoring her apology. "He's the oldest?"

"No, that would be Kade. He's here in Crooked Tree. Actually, he's my half-brother from a woman Pop was with before he met my mom." Sam lowered her gaze, stroking her cast. "The thing is, I met Kade's mother at Matt and Cassie's wedding. Her name is Reyna and she's really nice. And beautiful."

"The truth is, all of us like Reyna." Skye bent down, setting a tray of sandwiches, chips, and cookies on the coffee table. "I've seen her a few times. She seems wonderful, genuine in a way our mother could never be. And when she looks at Pop…" She bit her lip to stop herself from saying more.

"I know, right? He looks at her the same way." Sam took the sandwich Skye held out and took a bite. "This is great. Anyway, I wonder if he'd ever consider seeing her again."

"Sean asked Pop the same question."

Sam's brows lifted. "Yeah? What did he say?"

"Something about too much time going by." Skye looked at Tucker sitting on the other end of the sofa, a sandwich in his hand. "Ignore us. I'm sure this must be boring."

"Nope. Family stuff isn't boring." Reaching down, he grabbed a chip, popping it into his mouth. "This is real nice of you, Skye. Feeding me and letting me stay a few days."

"Why are you in town, Tucker? The last email said you were still working in Seattle." Sam studied her sandwich, not shifting her gaze to his.

"Too big a city. Too much traffic. Too many people who didn't seem to care about much, except money. Take your pick."

Setting her food down, Sam studied his face. "You quit?"

He nodded. "Yep. I found out it wasn't for me. I took a job with Maverick West here in Crooked Tree."

"You're kidding. They're like the biggest outdoor clothing manufacturer in the country."

Tucker chuckled. "Not quite, Sam. Third, but they're aiming to be number one. It's one reason they hired me. I'll be working on expanding the brand, establishing new distribution channels, and working with the product development group. I start tomorrow. They already have me scheduled to meet with some bigwig executive about a branding partnership. It all happened so fast, I haven't had a chance to find a place to live."

"Well, you have a room as long as you want. It's next to Sean's old room, down that hall." She nodded toward it, ignoring Sam's stunned expression.

"Thanks, Skye, but I don't want to impose."

"Not at all. It's Sam, Rhett, and me in this huge house. Sean has been transferred to another division, and Pop's in Fire Mountain. We have a ton of space."

"If you're sure. I haven't even had a chance to look for an apartment, and this sure beats living out of a motel."

Skye's cell phone rang before she had a chance to respond. "Hello?"

"Hey, Skye. It's Gage. I wondered if you'd have dinner with me tonight."

Chapter Six

Gage held the phone to his ear, hearing the deafening silence on the other end. It had been a mistake to call her, especially after he'd promised himself to stay away, scuttle whatever they'd started.

"Skye, are you there?"

"Um, yes…I'm here. Where are you?"

"Last minute trip to Crooked Tree. Ivan scheduled a meeting for me with some new guy at a local company. They want to talk about some kind of branding program, tying clothing to Double Ace." Pausing, he waited for her to respond. When she didn't, Gage rubbed the back of his neck, accepting this had been a bad idea. "Look, no problem if it's not enough notice or you're not interested."

"No. It's fine. I guess I'm a little surprised to hear from you. I'd like to see you. Tell me what time and where?"

Letting out a breath, he came up with the only place he could remember. "The last time I was here, Kade mentioned a place called Juan Diego's. Does seven o'clock work for you?"

"Works great. Same ol' thing? Boots and jeans?"

The image made Gage laugh. "Perfect. I'll see you then." He hung up, a sense of relief washing over him, which confused him even more. For two weeks, he'd spent more time at the office than usual, coming in at six in the morning, not leaving until after ten at night. Weekends had been the same. Whenever his thoughts shifted to Skye, he'd been able to ignore them, believing it best for both of them to forget their time in Houston. It was certainly best for her.

Scrubbing his face with both hands, he sighed. Gage could admit to missing her, wanting her in a way he'd never felt for any woman. The basic facts hadn't changed. He still had no use for anything permanent. He'd also had his fill of one-night stands, random hook ups, and pushy women.

All he wanted was something easy with a woman he liked, could consider a friend. He hated the term *friends with benefits*, but it defined what he needed better than anything else. He had to be careful, though. His feelings couldn't go deeper, and neither could Skye's. Whatever else happened, when it ended, they needed to walk away without scars or blame.

"Are you all right, Skye?"

She glanced at Sam's worried expression, forcing a smile. "Great. That was a friend I haven't heard from in a while. He wants to meet for dinner tonight."

"He?" Sam's brow arched.

"Yes, a male *friend*. And don't be reading more into it." She grabbed a chip, stuffing it into her mouth. "Will you two be okay here tonight?"

Sam rolled her eyes. "I think we'll find a way to manage. We do have food in the fridge, right?"

Tucker finished the last bite of his sandwich, holding up a hand. "If needed, I can head to the store, Skye. You go have a good time with your friend. If something comes up, Sam will call you."

"If you're sure."

"Do whatever you need to do, Skye. Tuck and I will be fine." Sam set down her bottle of water, then looked back at her sister. "Who is this friend anyway?"

Skye hesitated a moment, having no desire to share details. "Just a friend." She started to pick up the empty tray, stopping when Tucker beat her to it.

"You made lunch. I'll clean up."

"Thanks. I do need to make a few calls and deal with some business before getting ready to leave."

"Then get at it." He smiled as he turned and headed for the kitchen.

"He seems like a great guy," Skye whispered.

Sam's gaze stopped following Tucker to focus on her hands clasped in her lap. She lowered her voice. "Yeah. He's the best."

Gage sat at the bar, nursing a whiskey while he waited. He'd ordered one for Skye, too. After half an hour, the ice melted in the glass, watering down the high-priced liquor. He didn't know why it surprised him to be stood up, except it hadn't happened in years, and he hadn't expected it from her.

Downing the last of his drink, he checked his phone one more time. No messages. No calls. Sliding it into a clip on his belt, Gage grabbed her whiskey, finishing it in a few gulps, wincing at the watery taste. Pulling out his wallet, he tossed some bills on the table, then stood. Before he could turn, he felt a hand on his shoulder.

"I'm so sorry, Gage. I got held up."

The resigned look on his face faded as he turned at Skye's voice. "I'd given up on you." Before he could think better of it, he leaned down, kissing her cheek. "Sit down. I'll get you a drink."

"I should've called."

"Yeah, you should have, but you didn't. Now you can tell me in person what happened." He ordered another round of whiskey on ice, picking his up, touching it to the rim of her glass. "For the record, I'm glad you showed up." His sincere smile and the genuine warmth in his voice had her stomach doing flips. It had been over two weeks and she missed him. No one else put her at ease the way he did.

She held her glass to her lips, then hesitated. "I'm glad you called." Taking a sip, she set the drink down, running a finger around the edge. "When you didn't respond to my text or email, I figured, well…"

Gage didn't look up from studying the liquid in his glass. He could lie, tell her he'd always meant to respond, or admit the truth. He'd never been much into deception.

"You would've figured right," he murmured, still not looking at her. "The truth is, I didn't plan to get back in touch." When he glanced at her, she wouldn't meet his gaze.

"Oh." He couldn't mistake the disappointment in her voice, or ignore the tightness in his chest. "Then tonight is about telling me you're not interested." She plastered a smile on her face, lifting her glass toward him. "At least you told me in person."

Wrapping his hand around hers, he brought her whiskey to his lips and took a sip. Swallowing, he leaned forward, touching his lips to hers.

"After a couple weeks without talking to you, hearing your voice, I realized I couldn't walk away. Not yet."

Skye told herself his admission should've made her feel better. Instead, his words reminded her if she went through with this, sex with no commitment or hope for anything more, he would eventually walk away. All the reasons she thought it a good idea at first, the same reasons he had for proposing it, fell away. For the first time, Skye realized she wanted more than casual sex and no strings with him.

At the same time, she'd never wanted a man as much as she wanted Gage. Perhaps she could take what he offered, enjoy the time they had together, and walk away with her heart intact. Licking her lips, she searched his face, making a decision.

"Are you telling me you still want to have some type of arrangement?"

"If you're still up for it. I don't want you to do anything you don't want to."

A humorless laugh escaped her lips. "Trust me. No one makes me do anything I don't want to do. I *do* want to make one modification to our agreement, though."

Gage turned fully toward her, saying nothing as he narrowed his gaze. After a moment, he nodded. "What do you want to change?"

She swallowed, taking a chance she knew may backfire in the worst way. "We go with your original request. I want to be able to see other people."

His eyes widened a moment before he reined in his features, getting them under control. Gage could feel his jaw tighten, the same as the knot in his stomach. He didn't want permanent, but he didn't know if he could deal with her seeing other men.

"Let me get this straight. We see each other when it works for both of us, casual, no commitment."

"And no drama," she added.

"Right. No drama. In addition, we're free to see other people. Does that cover it?" His voice had gone from warm and inviting to cold and aloof.

"It's what you wanted, Gage. The more I've thought about it, I have to agree. You know, since we know nothing will ever develop between us."

This wasn't what he expected from Skye. She always seemed the type to fall in love, commit, be loyal to one man. Perhaps he'd misjudged her. Still, he couldn't help feeling as if he were being played. Well, two could play at this, and he wouldn't give Skye time to change her mind.

Swallowing the last of his whiskey, he set the glass down on the bar. "Done. Shall we start tonight?"

"Mr. Templeton, your table is ready."

They both looked at the hostess, a smile on her face, two menus in her hand.

Gage threaded his fingers through Skye's, feeling a shiver go through her. "The lady and I won't be needing the table. Please give it to someone else."

Skye could feel her body tremble as Gage opened the door to his hotel room, drawing her inside. He hadn't let go of her hand since helping her out of her truck. She'd followed him, wanting to have the ability to leave if she changed her mind.

They'd no more than made it inside the room when he kicked the door closed, pushed her up against the wall, and captured her mouth. The intensity of the kiss sparked a wave of intense heat, burning through her as if she were on fire. She'd never felt anything as potent as his body aligned against hers, hard muscles to her soft curves.

Wrapping her arms around him, her fingers played with the long hairs at the back of his neck before tugging him closer. A deep groan escaped as his lips scorched a path down her neck to the hollow of her throat before returning to recapture her mouth.

Without breaking the kiss, his hand came between them, unbuttoning her blouse, drawing it open and off her shoulders. His hands were everywhere—stroking her back and arms, then resting on her waist to tug her closer.

"I can't wait any longer, Skye," he breathed against her lips an instant before lifting her against his chest. Carrying her to the bed, he placed her in the center, pulling his shirt over his head, letting it drop to the floor. "Last chance, sweetheart. You can still walk away." The look on his face told her it would cost him if she changed her mind.

Rising onto her elbows, she let her gaze settle on the hard planes of his face, then wander down to the chiseled muscles of his chest and arms. She licked her lips, not even considering walking away.

Turning to her side, she sighed, reaching out her hand. "I'm not going anywhere, cowboy."

"I think that's your phone, sweetheart." Gage's raspy, sleep-filled voice whispered against her cheek as he tightened his hold around her, pulling her back against his chest. Kissing the soft spot below her ear, his lips continued to glide down her neck to her shoulder.

"That feels so good." Skye squirmed closer, ignoring the phone, focusing on the man behind her. She could feel the deep rumble in his chest as he chuckled.

"It's supposed to, darlin'. No use doing it otherwise." His hands began a slow procession over her hips, then stopped. "I don't think whoever is calling is going to give up."

He was right. She knew who it was. Could tell by the ring.

"It's Sam. I'm not ready to talk to her yet." She glanced at the clock, cringing at the hour. They'd made love so many times, she'd lost count. She knew she should have been home hours ago.

Gage supported himself on one arm, leaning over her. "It's five o'clock. She's probably worried. Maybe you should answer it." He loosened his grip, placing one more kiss on her shoulder.

Skye slid out of bed, already missing the warmth of his body against hers. Walking across the room, she glanced over her shoulder, a smile crossing her face when she saw Gage watching her.

"Hi, Sam."

"Skye? Where are you? You never came home."

She felt a slight tinge of guilt at the worry in her sister's voice. "I stayed with a friend." Skye glanced at Gage, then turned away. "Is something wrong?"

"No, not really."

"I'll be home in a little bit. Can I stop and pick up something for you and Tucker for breakfast?" She could hear Sam's deep sigh on the other end.

"Tucker went out last night and bought a ton of food. I don't know how we'll ever finish it all. Stay with your friend as long as you want. I just needed to know you were all right."

"I am, and I'll be home soon. Love you, Sam."

"Love you, too."

Skye set the phone down, shifting around to see Gage walking toward her. "As I thought, it was Sam." She walked into his outstretched arms, letting her face rest against his chest. They felt perfect together. Too perfect.

"She was worried."

"Yes, but it's all fine now."

"Good. I don't want us seeing each other to cause problems between you and your family." Gage kissed her before she could respond, taking his time, enjoying the feel of her in his arms. Groaning, he pulled away. "I have to shower and get to my meeting. I'm flying out right after."

His statement held no hint of regret, as if the last hours meant nothing. Time for both of them to get on with their lives.

"I'll get dressed and be out of here by the time you're done." Skye turned away, trying to push aside the ache, knowing it was stupid to feel any remorse. She'd accepted the arrangement and any consequences from it.

He reached for her, but she moved away. "Why don't you shower with me?"

"No. It's best if I leave and let you get ready. I never intended to stay the night." Spotting her clothes on the floor by the bed, she walked past him, not allowing herself to look up.

"Skye…"

She slipped on her jeans and blouse, doing her best to ignore the ball of tension in her stomach. "It's fine, Gage. We had a wonderful night. At least I did. Let me know when you get back up this way, and I'll do the same if I need to go to Houston." She felt a sense of triumph at the control in her voice.

He walked up to her, keeping his arms at his sides. "It was an amazing night, Skye. One of the best of my life." Reaching out, he stroked her arm, lifting her chin with a finger. "I'm looking forward to a lot more of them." Bending, he kissed her. "We'll see each other next week in Cold Creek. After Sam's accident, Kade rescheduled our meeting. I thought it was a good time to take a couple extra days off."

Her eyes softened, her mouth curving up at the corners. "Maybe I can do the same."

"We're staying at the same hotel. I'll try to get connecting rooms." He glanced at his phone when the alarm sounded. "I'd better get moving. This is my first meeting with this company."

Settling her hands on his shoulders, she placed a soft kiss on his mouth. Stepping around him, Skye grabbed her purse. Smiling, she rested a hand on the doorknob. "Hope it goes well, Gage. I'll see you next week."

Gage cursed the instant she closed the door behind her, already regretting the deal with Skye. Not because he didn't want her.

He'd thought last night and maybe a couple more would satisfy them both and they'd move on, forget their time together ever happened. The fallacy in his thinking hit him square in the chest. Although he suspected it, now he knew for certain—Skye was real trouble.

Stepping into the shower, he turned the knob, getting the water as hot as he could stand before placing both hands on the wall and letting it sluice down his back. He'd tried to make it about sex and nothing more. The problem, as he saw it, was he'd already formed a friendship with Skye, liked her a great deal, felt a connection he couldn't shake.

She should've been the last person he approached. Instead, Skye had sunk her claws right into him, making her the only woman he wanted. Now he had to deal with the fact all she wanted was sex—and to see other men. Worse, he'd walked right into it.

Cursing again, he grabbed the soap, washing away her scent. Gage already missed her, wanted nothing more than to pick up the phone and hear her voice. Slamming a hand against the shower wall, he cursed himself for ever coming up with such a stupid idea. He had no one to blame but himself.

Chapter Seven

Cold Creek, Colorado

"It's been much too long since we've had a chance to do this." Skye leaned back in her chair, sipping a mango margarita. She didn't usually go for the overly sweet drink. Tonight was an exception.

"We all have too much going on. Plus, you're way up north. It's a little tough to get together for happy hour." Cassie took a quick glance at Janie, her best friend since college, hoping tonight would help pull her out of the depression she'd been mired in for months. Ever since her firefighter fiancé, or ex-fiancé, had been badly hurt in a fire, she'd gone through the motions each day with no sign of the vivacious, outgoing woman everyone knew.

"There is that." Skye wished they could work closer to each other. Even though Kade led the bucking stock division, bulls remained in Crooked Tree, while the horses used in the bareback and saddle bronc events were kept in Cold Creek. "I heard a rumor the brothers were considering consolidating stock in one location." She referred to the three elder MacLarens, Heath, Jace, and Rafe.

Cassie shook her head and snorted. "When hell freezes over. I don't think they'll ever agree on where to merge the stock. Rafe won't budge from his position of keeping the bulls in Montana, and my father is just as adamant about keeping the horse stock in Cold Creek. Plus, Jace wants to keep the pleasure riding horse business in Fire Mountain."

"Sounds like a stalemate."

Skye and Cassie turned to Janie, who'd been quiet until now. No one could understand why Kurt Dobson had called it off between them. They'd been crazy about each other, planning a wedding a few months after Matt and Cassie's. Janie didn't care about the burns or extensive rehabilitation he'd have to endure. All she wanted was Kurt, but he'd shut her out, the same as he'd done with many of his friends.

"Janie, if you could choose one of the three places, where would it be?" Cassie knew she'd go anyplace, as long at Matt was with her.

"You know I can't leave Cold Creek." Janie took a slow sip of her martini, twisting the stem between her fingers.

"How's Kurt doing?"

"The same, Skye. At least that's what I hear. He's had several rounds of skin grafts, goes to physical therapy, and pretty much keeps to himself." She sighed, her drink shaking in her hand. "He still refuses to see me. His closest friend, Jerrod James, took me to dinner last week." She swallowed, forcing the words out. "He said Kurt wants me to stop trying to contact him. He said I should *get a life*, one without him."

Cassie leaned over, laying a hand on Janie's arm. "That's ridiculous, and so unlike Kurt."

Janie shrugged. "Maybe unlike the Kurt who asked me to marry him. According to Jerrod, he's changed."

"It's the burns, Janie. Given enough time, he'll come around."

"How much time, Cassie? I'd wait forever if I knew he still cared even a little about me. My parents want me to come home, find a job back east. I can't. I'm not ready to give up on him." She twisted the engagement ring on her left hand.

"Does he still know you wear your engagement ring?" Skye asked, her throat tightening at the pain in Janie's face.

"Jerrod told him. Said Kurt told him I should pawn it because there'll never be a wedding band to go with it." Janie swiped the dampness from her face. "Sorry. I keep thinking I won't let it get to me."

"Do you want us to go to his house and knock some sense into him?"

Janie knew Cassie was only partially joking. "If only. Jerrod and several of the guys at the fire station offered the same." She let out a deep breath. "Enough about me and my miserable love life. How about you, Skye? I already know Cassie is sickeningly happy in her marriage."

"It's true. I am." Cassie laughed, signaling the waitress for more drinks.

Even after a week, Skye still shivered each time she thought about Gage and their night together. If all went as planned, she'd be with him tomorrow night, and maybe the next.

"Nothing special. Work, family." She shrugged.

"Good evening, ladies."

Skye, Cassie, and Janie turned in their seats to see three men, each holding a drink and wearing cocky grins.

"Gentlemen. Can we help you with something?" Cassie flashed a bright smile, but anyone who knew her could detect the irritation in her eyes.

The tallest of the three stepped forward, making eye contact with each of them, settling his gaze on Skye. "My friends and I would like to buy you drinks."

"That's very kind of you, but we just ordered another round." Cassie held up her glass.

"Then maybe we can join you." He rested his hand on the back of her chair.

Cassie glanced behind him, a wide smile breaking out on her face. "I'm sorry, but I believe those chairs are about to be taken."

Skye turned in the direction of Cassie's gaze, her jaw dropping open when she saw Gage, Matt, and Kade coming up behind them.

"Hello, ladies. Sorry we kept you waiting." Matt placed his hands on Cassie's shoulders before bending down for a kiss. Straightening, he looked at the three guys standing there, acting as if they didn't quite know what to do. "Sorry, fellas. These women are already taken."

"Can't blame us," the tall one said before turning away.

"I can't blame them at all," Gage mumbled. He didn't hesitate to claim the chair next to Skye, his eyes locked on hers. "How've you been, Skye?"

Her tongue darted out to moisten her lips. "Fine...I'm fine. I, uh...heard you weren't coming to town until tomorrow."

Gage almost chuckled at her obvious discomfort. He'd wanted to surprise her. It appeared he had. "Wrapped things up in Houston a little early and managed to catch a flight out. When Matt said he and Kade were meeting you here, I sort of invited myself along."

"Not true. Kade and I insisted he come." Matt settled next to Cassie, draping an arm around her shoulders.

"As I recall, it didn't take much convincing." Kade took a seat next to Janie. "You ladies set for drinks, or can I order you more?"

"Already done," Cassie answered a moment before the waitress walked up. Setting down the drinks, she took the men's order and moved off.

"How are you doing, Janie?" Kade knew Kurt still refused to see her. He'd seen the same more than once while in Special Forces. Men wanting to pull into themselves, pretend those they loved didn't exist.

"Same. Work is crazy. My boss is a real taskmaster." She shot a look at Matt, then smiled.

"I agree," Cassie added. "A real slave driver."

"Hey, you two," Matt objected. "Remember who's paying for dinner tonight."

"Kade," Cassie, Janie, and Skye said in unison, laughing.

"Fine, but don't think I'll forget this when it's time for your reviews." Matt's eyes gleamed, a sly smile on his face.

Skye continued to half-listen to the banter, more than a little aware of Gage's thigh resting against hers. Placing a hand on her stomach, she tried to quell the butterflies that refused to still.

"How was your week?"

She glanced over, seeing Gage's heated gaze on her. "Busy. I had to pack a lot into the last few days in order to make these meetings."

"That so? Was there a doubt you'd be able to join us?" His gaze narrowed, one brow lifting in question.

She let out a shaky breath, a smile curving her lips. "No. Not really."

His face softened. "Good. I'm glad to hear it."

"What are you two talking about? It must be better than the discussion we're having over here about the new contracts." Cassie leaned into Matt, her words directed at Skye and Gage.

Gage grinned. "Same as you. Rodeos we should go after, who we're competing against."

Skye bit her lip, listening to the lie roll off his lips. Her stomach tightened, warning her how easy it would be to get caught up in this man, letting desire rule her common sense. She wondered if he'd be able to lie to her as easily. Feeling him watching her, she glanced over, surprised to see his brows furrow in question.

"Who's hungry?" Matt stood, holding out his hand to Cassie. "'Cause I'm starved."

As in the bar, Gage took the seat next to Skye, holding out her chair, letting his arm brush against hers. She didn't know what she'd been thinking when agreeing to their arrangement. If her family didn't guess what was going on between them, she'd be shocked. By the time they finished dessert, which Kade always insisted on having, her nerves were fried.

"What time tomorrow?" Gage rested a hand on the small of Skye's back for an instant as they all walked away from the table. He'd have left it longer if she hadn't sent him a withering glare.

"Eight, if that works for you." Matt held the door open, letting the others walk past him.

"Works fine. Skye, do you need a ride to the hotel?"

"She's with me, Gage. We'll see you in the morning." Kade pulled out his keys, waiting until Skye walked up beside him. Once they were in his car, he started the engine, glancing at her. "Do you want to tell me what's going on with you and Gage?"

Her eyes widened for an instant, her hands tightening on her lap. "Gage and I? I don't know what you mean."

He almost laughed at her inability to lie. During his time as an undercover DEA agent, he'd become adept at knowing when someone told the truth. She didn't pass the test.

"Sorry, sweetheart, but you're a lousy liar."

Her mouth opened, then shut, before she shifted to stare out the side window.

"Look, if there's something going on between you two, it's your business. You're my sister. I just want to make sure you know what you're getting into with Gage."

She swung back toward him. "What do you mean?"

"Don't get me wrong. Gage is a great guy, a hard worker, and from what I've seen, honest." Kade let out a slow breath, as if deciding how much more to say. "Matt's as close to Gage as anyone. He'd no doubt tell you to stay away from him."

Her throat worked, trying to dislodge the lump Kade's words created. "Why would he have a problem with it?"

"Because Gage is a player. The man has no intention of committing to one woman and settling down."

"From what I've heard, you were the same."

A smile split his face. "I was until I met Brooke."

"Mitch was the same. Look what happened when he met Dana." She hated the hope she heard in her words.

"Is that what you're thinking? That you'll be able to change him, make him want to settle down?" He almost wished he'd kept his mouth shut when her face sobered and shoulders slumped.

Skye shook her head, her voice lowering to a whisper. "It's not like that between us, Kade."

"So you're not involved?"

She let out a deep sigh. "I won't lie to you. All I can say is we're both going into this with our eyes open."

Kade shook his head, mumbling a curse. "You know, if he hurts you, I'll have to kill him."

Skye snorted, her eyes clouding with emotion. "Thanks, big brother, but you don't have to worry. I'm a big girl. I know exactly the kind of man Gage is. I'll be okay."

He nodded as he parked the car at the hotel. "I'm going to hold you to that."

Sitting on the edge of her bed, Skye stared at the extra key card Gage had given her. She knew he'd be waiting, expecting her to come to him. If it weren't for Kade's warning, she would've already been in his room, probably in his bed.

She didn't know how much time had passed before a soft knock sounded at her door.

"Skye, open up."

Gage. He'd come to her.

"Come on, sweetheart. Don't make me wait out here all night."

For some reason, she knew he would. Standing, she took the few steps to the door and pulled it open.

He wasted no time slipping past her, taking her in his arms, lowering his mouth to hers. She barely had time to think, melting against him, letting Gage take control. Wrapping her arms around him, she moaned into his mouth, getting a groan of satisfaction in return. In an instant, he'd lifted her in his arms and walked to the bed, sitting down, adjusting her on his lap. Looking over his shoulder, he spotted the extra key card.

"Are you going to tell me why you didn't come to my room?"

She shook her head. "Kade knows."

He stilled, letting the words sink in. "How?"

"I don't know. I swear he has a sixth sense about people."

It didn't take Gage long to piece together what had been said. "Let me guess. He warned you away from me."

"Yeah, pretty much. Actually, he said he'd have to kill you if you hurt me."

Gage's deep, rich laughter helped Skye relax. "Kill me, huh?"

"Yep. That's what he said."

His fingers began working the buttons on her blouse as he feathered kisses along her face and down her neck. "Then I guess I'd better not give him any reason to get mad." Shifting, he settled her back on the bed, stretching out beside her. "I've thought of little except this all week, Skye. Are you going to let me stay?"

Slipping her arms around his neck, she smiled. "If you still want to."

"There's no place I'd rather be."

Skye woke at sunrise the next morning, already knowing if she rolled over, Gage would be gone. Sitting up, she scanned the room, finding no sign he'd ever been there. Part of her was glad he didn't want them to get caught together. Still, she felt her heart constrict at the way he'd fled without waking her.

Taking her time in the shower, letting the hot water flow over her body, she thought of the night before, wishing he hadn't felt the need to leave. Nothing would feel better right now than Gage next to her, running his hands down her body as steam filled the bathroom.

Again, Kade's warning filled her thoughts. Skye knew he meant well and didn't want to see her get hurt, the same as Matt or anyone in the family. They watched out for and protected each other, which she found endearing, albeit sometimes stifling. Sharing the house with Sam and Rhett didn't help. She couldn't make a move without one of them asking her about it. In addition, their father made it difficult to justify moving out. He made the payments, not accepting anything from them, other than they take care of the place in his absence. He might leave Fire Mountain someday, although his return to Crooked Tree seemed further and further away with each passing month.

Wrapping herself in a towel more suited for a child, she combed and dried her hair, still unable to push Gage from her thoughts. It wouldn't be long before their meeting. She had no doubt he'd take a spot beside her. Skye anticipated his closeness, at the same time worrying about how Kade might react. She hadn't asked him to keep what he knew to himself, yet somehow knew he would.

Her stomach rumbled, reminding her she needed food before facing the morning. Grabbing her purse, the key card to her room and the one to Gage's, she headed downstairs. From her last visit, she remembered the complimentary breakfast of cold cereal, half-frozen rolls, and congealed gravy with biscuits. Today, she spotted a bowl of sliced fresh fruit and went straight toward it.

"Join us?"

Startled at the familiar voice, the one that had whispered in her ear much of the night, she glanced over her shoulder. Gage and Kade sat together, both with their eyes trained on her. She cringed, wondering if Kade had said anything to Gage. Shoving down the dread tightening her chest, she walked over, slinging her purse over the back of a chair.

"Good morning. You two must have gotten up early."

"We were both heading downstairs for our morning run at the same time." Kade cast a quick look between her and Gage. "Did you sleep well?"

Tucking a strand of hair behind her ear, she could feel her face heat at the implication in his words. "Great. As soon as I have some coffee and food, I'll be ready for today."

Gage watched her, his face a mask. Even though Skye had warned him, Kade mentioning her during their run had blindsided him. His voice had been friendly. The message wasn't.

As far as Kade was concerned, screwing around with his sister didn't cut it. If Gage was in it for what he could get, he'd better back off and let her go.

Gage had wanted to object, tell Kade he had it all wrong, that he cared a great deal about Skye. The question was how much? Enough to turn a casual relationship into a real one? They'd been together twice. Neither could know how it would roll out over the following weeks and months, whether their feelings would grow or fade. In the end, Gage told Kade he'd have to trust that he and Skye were adults and could deal with any fallout from being together. Kade didn't like it, but he hadn't pushed further.

Watching Skye walk toward them, a plate of fruit in one hand, coffee in the other, Gage knew he had to make a decision. Jeopardizing the partnership with the MacLarens wasn't an option. Neither was hurting Skye. As much as he hated to admit it, Kade had been right to warn him off. Skye had a bright future, could have any man she wanted. She didn't need to be saddled with a worn-out cowboy who had no intention of ever getting roped into anything serious.

Sipping his coffee, ignoring the pain slicing through him, Gage came to a decision. They had one more night in Cold Creek. One more time together. He'd make it good for her, then end it.

Feeling a punch to his gut as she smiled at him before taking a bite of fruit, Gage steeled himself, realizing one more night might even be too much. Neither could afford to get in any deeper. He'd change his flight to leave that afternoon. Somehow, doing what he thought was right never felt so wrong.

Chapter Eight

Reading the text, Skye's heart seized, all the air leaving her lungs.

"Are you all right?" Cassie stood next to her, seeing confusion cloud her face.

Biting her lip, Skye nodded. "Yes. I'm, um…I'm fine." She walked out the door at the Cold Creek offices, stopping when she realized Kade was her ride back to the hotel.

The team meeting with Gage had gone well, ending with him leaving for the hotel, the rest of them continuing with other business. They had plans to meet for dinner at a remote restaurant, then Skye would spend the night in his room.

Instead, she stared at a text. Gage had taken a flight back to Houston that afternoon and couldn't meet her as planned. He didn't know when he'd be able to see her again.

"That's it," she mumbled as she wandered around the parking lot, unable to focus on anything other than his terse message. Skye's instincts told her something had been off when she saw him at breakfast. Instead of the heated gazes he usually sent her, the discreet touches she expected, his face was devoid of expression, his gaze fixed on anything except her. Rereading his text for the fourth time, she felt a sharp pain slice through her.

Skye scolded herself. He'd been called back to work. She shouldn't read anything more into it. His abrupt words were typed as he dashed to the hotel, then airport, attempting to catch a flight.

All her instincts insisted her excuses for him were a lie. He'd called it off, not having the guts to do it in person.

"I'm so stupid." This time, her words were louder, laced with anger.

"Are you talking to me?"

Spinning around, she saw Kade come up behind her, his smile fading when he saw her face. Placing a hand on her shoulder, he said nothing, waiting   .

Shaking her head and stepping away, she slid the phone into her purse. "Talking to myself. So, are you ready to head to the hotel?"

"Yeah. Climb on in."

They rode back in a thick silence neither seemed inclined to break. Skye stared out her window, Kade focused on the road ahead. She wanted to reply to Gage's text, find out the real reason for his quick departure, and make him tell her it was over. She didn't.

Settling a hand on her stomach, a wave of fear took over. The truth was, she didn't want to know. Didn't want to face the fact two nights with her had been enough.

"Skye?" Kade's voice, his hand on her arm, pulled her from her thoughts.

"Huh?"

"We're at the hotel."

She hadn't noticed one thing about the trip back. "Oh, right." Stepping out of the car, she followed him through the lobby and to the elevator.

"We're supposed to meet the others for dinner at seven."

"If you have no objection, I'll order in. I have a lot of work to catch up on." She didn't meet his gaze.

"You gonna tell me what's wrong?"

The elevator reached her floor as he spoke, the door sliding open. Stepping into the hall, she turned back as the doors began to close.

"It's over. Gage left."

Gage massaged the back of his neck, trying to fortify himself for the mess awaiting him in Houston. Gonzo's call had been brief. Homeland Security had shown up early that morning, searching the premises and checking identification. Ivan had already been notified and would be arriving early afternoon. If Gage hadn't been in meetings with MacLaren, shutting down his phone out of courtesy, he'd already be in Houston handling damage control.

Instead, he'd been taking notes, giving his opinion on various rodeo opportunities, and trying to come up with the best way to break it off with Skye. Even now, his stomach clenched at what had to be done.

By now, she'd seen his text, knew he wouldn't be meeting her. Gage hadn't planned for it to happen this way—by text, email, or phone. He'd wanted to talk to her in person, alone, so she could tell him to go to hell in private. Whatever she said wouldn't come close to what he deserved.

He'd told her the truth, saying he didn't know when they'd see each other again. What waited for him in Houston could change everything, tie up his time for hours, days, or weeks. At some point, he had to face her. It was what a man did.

"May I get you anything to drink?"

His gaze lifted to the pretty flight attendant with a smile almost as bright as Skye's. His throat constricted with the knowledge he might never again be the object of her smile or the desire he saw each time he looked into her eyes.

"Sir?"

"Uh…no, thank you."

Glancing back out the window, he allowed himself time to think about her. No woman had ever captured his attention so completely or had him figuring ways to get her alone. He wondered if it had really been his decision to let her go, or had Kade's warning goaded him into it?

"The captain has turned on the seat belt sign…"

He tuned out the rest of the announcement, knowing it by heart after so much time traveling.

Forcing himself to push Skye from his thoughts, he reviewed the list he'd started of what needed to be accomplished when he got back. Not for the first time, he thought of Gonzo, thankful the man worked for him. Without his quick thinking and steady temperament, who knew what damage may have occurred when the federal agents appeared.

Assuming the press got wind of the raid, they needed to come up with a communication plan for clients and partners. They couldn't afford to have their closest allies believe Double Ace was involved in or condoned any illegal activities. His jaw tightened when he thought of Ivan's father and uncles. They wouldn't tolerate actions threatening their business empire or casting them in a bad light. Whatever happened next would be crucial to not only Double Ace's future, but his and Ivan's.

"Did they find anything?" Gage pushed through the door of his office, Gonzo right behind him, shutting the door.

"No, boss. They weren't specific about what they were looking for, but my guess is drugs."

"And the employees?"

"All their documentation is current and the forms we have on file correct." Gonzo shifted in his chair, glancing around the room, not meeting Gage's eyes. "I'm sorry, boss. I should've known something like this would happen."

Gage's body stilled. "How do you figure?"

"The industry we're in and the workers we employ. We're a target. At some point, they were bound to sweep down on us, if for no other reason than they can." Taking off his hat, he ran a hand through his short black hair.

"I hear what you're saying, but they don't waste manpower unless they have probable cause. Someone gave them a reason to check us out." Gage had thought the same the minute he'd seen Gonzo's text. What bothered him most was the possibility someone inside Double Ace had contacted the feds. But who, and why? "What happened when they left?"

"The agent in charge left this card." Gonzo pulled it from his pocket, handing it to Gage. "He said you could call with questions. At least there were only six agents, not the dozen or more I've heard about from others who've been raided."

Gage let out a slow breath as he glanced through the window to the pens below. "Did the press come by or call?"

Gonzo's brows furrowed. "Now that you mention it, no. At least not that I've heard, but I stayed in the back when the agents checked the property. The office manager and Daria stayed inside with the agent reviewing the paperwork." He started to stand. "I'll check with Daria."

Gage held up a hand for him to sit back down, pushing a button on the desk phone.

"Yes, Gage?"

"Any calls from the press, Daria?"

"No, sir."

"If you *do* get any, or they come by asking about the visit by the federal agents, get in touch with me. Any questions?"

"Do you want to take the calls or call them back?"

"Take a message and I'll call them back after Mr. Santiago arrives." He clicked off, his thoughts still caught up on who would place a call to Homeland Security. "Did they have dogs?"

Gonzo nodded. "And a search warrant. I don't know how they got one. I thought they had to have some pretty solid evidence before one was granted."

"So did I." Gage focused on the agent's card for the first time, not recognizing the name. Not that he would. His experience in this area didn't amount to anything. "For now, get on out with the workers. The sooner we get back to normal, the better."

Moving to the door, Gonzo stopped. "Ivan should be here within the hour. All I did was notify him of what was happening. He didn't say anything to me about what he planned to do."

"I'm sure he'll have some thoughts by the time he arrives. And thanks, Gonzo. You did great."

A sad look crossed the man's face before he opened the door and left. Gage wished he would have been here, but there wasn't much more he could've done, other than talk to the agent in charge. From what he could tell, Gonzo handled it well, offering assistance and not panicking.

At least the press hadn't been alerted. Of course, that didn't mean they still wouldn't rear their heads, try to make something out of nothing.

"Hey, Gage. I wondered when you'd call."

"And why would that be, Thad?" Waiting for Ivan to arrive, Gage sat at his desk, talking to his good friend, Thad Montgomery.

"I heard about the raid. Also heard they found nothing."

"Hell, Montgomery. How could you know about it when it just happened this morning?"

"I've got my sources."

"And you didn't think to notify me?" Gage's temper rose.

"If I'd have known ahead of time, I would've given you a heads-up. Unfortunately, I heard about it during a lunch meeting. Cost me a dinner and whiskey to get my source to call me afterward with an update. He didn't say much, just that there were no arrests. You may have dodged a bullet on this one, man."

Gage's senses went on alert. "Why's that?"

"Look. I don't want to talk about this on the phone. Get in touch tomorrow and we'll meet at the usual place. Oh, by the way, your man Gonzalez?"

"What about him?"

"He stayed right with me when I brought the dog and handler by. Never got more than a few feet away from me."

"So? He's the stock manager. What happens in the yards is part of his job."

"Forget I said anything. Too many years living with paranoia. Call me tomorrow and we'll set up a time." Thad hung up, leaving Gage with an unpleasant sense of dread.

A minute later, Daria buzzed him.

"Gage, Mr. Santiago is here."

"Thanks, Daria. I'll be right down." He thought once more of the mixed signals he got from Thad, then pushed them aside. All his focus had to be on what happened today, how to reduce any damage and prevent future visits from the government.

Gage tapped his pen on the desk, watching Ivan pace back and forth in front of the window. They'd gone over the information Gonzo had given. As far as Ivan knew, his father and uncles hadn't heard of the raid. He stopped pacing, taking a seat across from Gage.

"It's been hours, and we've heard nothing from the press. As comforting as that is, my family will learn of what happened and demand answers." Ivan's expression didn't change as he spoke. He had the enviable ability to give little away when under pressure. "If we've still heard nothing by tomorrow, I'll fly back to León, tell them in private, and assure them nothing came of it. Is there any reason to call the federal agent who left his card?"

"They found nothing—in the yards or the files. No notice of any kind. I doubt the agent would tell us anything, such as if we are still on some agency list or what information they used to secure a search warrant." Gage stood, stretching his arms to relieve the tightness. "I recommend we leave it alone for now."

Ivan steepled his fingers under his chin, nodding. "I want four men posted for each delivery from Mexico. Two men for the driver and two if there's someone riding along. They're to report anything suspicious to you personally."

"Not Gonzo?"

Ivan looked up. "No. *You* directly. I want everyone else to keep doing their jobs, as if nothing happened."

Gage nodded, glancing out the window behind him. "I don't like any of this. Someone is feeding the feds a load of crap about us, and I can't help but believe it's someone connected with Double Ace."

"My uncles and father have many enemies. The list is too long to mention, although it is safe to say any one of them would like nothing more than to bury my family. Even with the agreements my uncles have made, hatred runs deep and memories last generations." Ivan shook his head, then stood. "No, my friend. I don't believe it is someone here. What would they have to gain?"

"Money?"

"Perhaps, but getting involved with the cartels is a dangerous game. There is no loyalty, no future. Those on the bottom are crushed like bugs for any misdeed. You have a loyal team. I wish mine back in León were as trustworthy."

Gage believed the same about the people who worked for him. "I'm certain you're right. There isn't a single person I'd suspect of doing anything to damage the company. I'll call our rodeo customers to check-in. If they've heard something, they won't hesitate to bring it up. How do you want me to handle the MacLarens?"

Ivan drew in a long breath. His aunt, Reyna, was Kade MacLaren's mother, although she and Rafe had never married. Anything involving the MacLarens was tricky.

"It would be best to stay with normal relations. You're the main contact. I'd like you to call Kade or Matt, see how the final agreements for the additional rodeos are coming. The drafts were approved by the family, so it's time to move forward."

"If Kade's heard anything?" Gage suspected Ivan knew he wouldn't lie.

"Tell him the truth. I'm certain you'll be able to come up with the right words to ease any concerns. It's doubtful he, or anyone else, has heard anything about it." Ivan pulled out his phone, checking the time. "I need to get back to the airport. It's important I meet with the family before someone else gets word to them."

"I'll let you know how the calls with the customers go."

Ivan walked to the door, resting his hand on the knob. "Do you have another meeting scheduled with the MacLarens?"

Gage's throat tightened at the thought of seeing Skye again. He knew they needed to talk in person. She deserved to hear the decision from his lips, not by reading an email or text. He just wasn't quite ready. "Not yet. Maybe not for a while."

Chapter Nine

Crooked Tree, Montana

"No problem at all. We can have a revised proposal to you in a couple days. It's always good news to hear about a rodeo expanding its days. I'll be in touch."

Skye hung up, making a few more notes before opening the original proposal for the rodeo in Oklahoma. It didn't take long to make the changes, increasing the number of days from two to three.

Printing the agreement, she walked next door to Kade's office. He motioned her inside as he finished a call.

"Do you have a minute to review an updated proposal?"

"Sure. Sit down and tell me what you've got."

A few minutes later, they'd reviewed the details, making a couple minor adjustments before Skye stood to leave.

"Are you doing okay?"

She knew Kade referred to her and Gage, but she didn't want to talk about it. The morning before, they'd sat in meetings, casting each other heated glances, trying to keep whatever they had going quiet. Then he'd left. He hadn't called, sent a text, or emailed since the initial message telling her he had to leave. In twenty-four hours, everything had changed.

"Okay. The worst part is I feel like such a fool." She shrugged, knowing Kade would be able to detect a lie. "And I've no one to blame but myself."

Kade lifted a brow. "How's that?"

"I don't take risks like you, Mitch, or most of the MacLarens. Gage never lied to me. I knew his terms and took a chance." Her lips twisted into a wry smile. "And, truthfully, I'm fine. It didn't last long enough for me to hurt much. Maybe taking a risk every once in a while isn't such a bad idea."

Kade rubbed the back of his neck. "I'm no expert on any of this stuff, but he could've had a legitimate reason for leaving. It's a busy time of year for us and Double Ace. I don't think Gage is the type of man who'd call it off without telling you why."

Skye didn't know how to respond. Gage didn't seem the type to her, either. "However it turns out, I won't let any of it affect the partnership we have."

"I never thought you would."

Houston

It had taken Gage most of the day to make a friendly call to each of his clients under the guise of keeping in touch. More than once, he'd been drawn into a long discussion about everything from rodeo stock questions to if he'd ever consider riding again. He just had one more call to make. The one he dreaded.

Punching in the MacLaren number, he told himself there wasn't any difference between this call and the ones he'd made all day.

"MacLaren Bucking Stock."

"It's Gage Templeton. I'd like to speak with Kade."

"He's on another line, but let me see if I can catch Skye."

Gage didn't have a chance to respond before hearing her voice.

"Skye MacLaren."

The lump in his throat became a painful knot at the sound of her voice.

"Hey. It's Gage."

The silence stretched a ridiculous amount of time before she responded.

"Hi, Gage. Did you need to speak with Kade?"

He took the phone off speaker, putting the handset to his ear. "I do need to talk to him. First, I owe you an apology for leaving like I did."

A few beats went by before she answered. "Not a problem. We agreed no strings, no drama."

He tried to ignore the strain in her voice telling him otherwise. "There are some things going on down here that need my attention. As soon as I can, I'd like to talk to you. In person, not over the phone."

Her stomach clenched. She already knew what he wanted to say, guessing it when she read his brief text. "Look, Gage, there's no need to make a special trip up here to talk. I'm not going to make this hard for you."

"Skye…"

"Just tell me you're over whatever happened between us so we can both move on."

"Skye, I'd rather—"

"Just say it." Her calm, resolute voice belied the unexpected pain gripping her heart.

Gage blew out a breath. He didn't want to talk about this over the phone, but she didn't seem inclined to do the same.

"All right then. You and me…it's probably not smart."

Skye let the words sink in. She had to give him credit. He seemed to be doing his best to let her down gently. Regardless, over was still over. Clearing her throat, she adjusted the phone against her ear.

"That wasn't so hard, was it?" A light tinge of hope laced her words, as if she wanted him to admit how difficult walking away was for him. She knew the thought would seem irrational to most. They'd known each other a few months, been together twice, agreeing to see other people. Yet she'd felt an instant connection with Gage, a desire unlike anything she ever thought possible. The idea of never being with him again caused unexpected physical pain, stronger than the hurt she felt when learning of her fiancé's betrayal.

He snorted. "Yeah, Skye, it *was* hard."

She didn't know how to respond to what seemed to be an admission of some kind. "Well, it's done." Her voice had lowered to a halting whisper. "Let me put you through to Kade."

"Skye…wait."

She let out a frustrated breath. "What, Gage?"

Even hundreds of miles away and over a phone line, he could hear the hurt in her voice. "We're good, right?"

The short laugh held no humor. Of course he'd be more concerned about the bottom line than anything else. "Don't worry. I won't let a couple nights together affect our business dealings. Double Ace will still make money, and so will we."

Without letting him respond, she punched in the number to transfer the call to Kade.

Setting down the phone, she gripped the edge of the desk with both hands, accepting it truly was over.

"At least it wasn't one and done." The whispered words came out a little more brittle than intended.

Sitting back in her chair, she closed her eyes, allowing herself one last memory of their final night together. They'd made love over and over until she couldn't move, then he'd wrapped his arms around her and pulled her close, his soft breath fanning her neck. Even now, a shiver ran through her.

It's a good memory to have, Skye told herself, not sure if she meant it, but determined to believe it.

Houston

"Dammit." Gage pinched the bridge of his nose, then slammed his hands on his desk.

The discussion with Kade had gone well, neither mentioning Skye. Like their other customers, Kade hadn't heard a word about the fed's visit the day before. They'd agreed on a meeting in Cold Creek in a few weeks, then ended the call.

The way things ended with Skye ate at him. He'd been the one to set the rules, insisting on not letting emotions complicate their time together. The fact they were good…no, great together shouldn't influence the need to keep any feelings out of it. Kade's warning should've given Gage a sense of relief, a way to end it with Skye before anything developed.

He choked out a harsh laugh. They'd been together twice, but he wasn't nearly done with her. An uneasy feeling wrestled within him when he realized he might never be done with her. Before Kade expressed his thoughts, Gage had every intention of seeing her again, and again whenever their schedules allowed. Then he'd crumbled at a few concerned words from Skye's brother. Did Kade really believe they would let their emotions destroy the hard-won success of the partnership?

Gage shook his head. As he thought through it, he believed Kade's words were meant as more of a warning not to hurt Skye than worry over the business. Right now, all he could feel was a deep ache in his own chest, making it hard to breathe. He wondered how he'd let a couple times with one woman mess up his carefully designed plan for passionate nights without attachment. At this moment, Gage felt more attached to Skye than any woman he'd ever known, including his faithless wife.

Within weeks, he'd fly to Cold Creek for one more meeting with the MacLarens. He needed to find some way of getting Skye to talk to him in private. After the call today, he knew it wouldn't be easy. Nothing about this entire situation was easy.

A knock on his door had Gage shifting his focus from a woman he couldn't purge from his thoughts to Daria, who sent him a killer smile. He knew she was in her early twenties. Pretty with a great figure, she'd done everything except come right out and invite him to share some time. He'd learned to recognize the not so sly glances, the body language, the way she got close to him with no encouragement. The rodeo circuit could be counted on for two things—tough rides and willing women.

Perhaps he was getting old, or growing up. Even the knockout in front of his desk didn't tempt him.

"What is it, Daria?"

She held out a piece of paper. "You were on the phone when this call came in."

Gage took it without reading the name. "You didn't have to bring this upstairs."

Daria trailed her fingers along his desk, glancing up at him through thick eyelashes.

He blew out a frustrated breath. "Daria…"

Straightening, she crossed her arms. "I know. Look at the name."

Gage sighed, glanced at the message, then frowned. *Brent.*

"He said he's your brother and it's important you call him back."

He set the note aside. "Thanks."

"You're welcome." She smiled again. "I don't have plans for dinner. I thought maybe…"

The perfect end to a crappy day, he thought, pushing up from the desk. "If you're asking me to have dinner with you, the answer is no."

"Oh. I see." She turned to leave.

"I don't date employees." He walked around the desk, coming up to stand a foot away from her, noting the way she'd clasped her hands in front of her. "You're a great employee, a real asset to Double Ace. I'd never put you or myself in an awkward situation by going out with you."

"I see." Her face flushed. "I thought…" Her voice trailed off. She didn't meet his gaze as she walked to the door.

"Are you going to be all right?"

She sucked in a breath. "Sure. I need this job, and you're a great boss. Sorry I overstepped."

"Forget it. We'll go on as if nothing happened."

An embarrassed smile crossed her face. "No problem. Well, it's after five. I guess I'll be going. Should I lock the front door?"

"Please. I'll be working for a while longer."

Gage waited until he heard the door at the bottom of the stairs close, indicating she'd returned to the front. He needed a couple aspirin, or a stiff drink.

The urge had been strong to tell Daria he was seeing someone. He hadn't. The fact it even crossed his mind couldn't have been more of a surprise. Dating or relationship didn't fit in his vocabulary, or his life. Somehow, when he thought of Skye, both words felt right.

Gage's stomach growled for the hundredth time. If he didn't stop pushing through the paperwork, by the time he grabbed something to eat, he wouldn't get home before midnight.

Dropping the pen, he rubbed his eyes, then took one more look at his desk. The stacks of files were shorter, his to-do list half as long as it had been when he started. Placing his hands on his desk, he started to stand, then settled back when his gaze landed on the phone message Daria had given him.

Brent.

His jaw hardened as he picked it up, reading it again. They hadn't spoken in four years, and Gage still felt no urge to call. Brent had told Daria it was important. Their parents would've called if one of them were sick or needed help. This had to be about Brent. Maybe he needed money or a place to stay while he looked for work. Even though he hadn't asked, their mother had told Gage he'd gone from one job to another, moving between several cities. Nothing had worked out.

The lump in his throat grew thick remembering how he'd always been the one to look out for his younger brother, stepping in when some random bully tried to push Brent around. The last time he'd seen him, Brent stood almost shoulder to shoulder with Gage. No one bullied him any longer.

Maybe he'd called to ask Gage to forgive him, as he'd done several times the year after the betrayal. After being rebuffed each time, he'd stopped.

Important. Gage couldn't find it in him to care. Wadding the message into a ball, he dropped it in the trash, determined to hold onto his hatred for as long as possible. It had consumed him the first year, lessened the second, then been ignored. *How ironic*, Gage thought. He'd never been in love with Gwen, and apparently, she'd never been in love with him. She'd loved being married to a rodeo star. Loved the life he'd provided while competing and afterward. It hadn't been enough for her. They'd spoken of divorce more than once, and even though he believed in the sanctity of marriage, he accepted it would happen at some point. In a way, finding Brent and Gwen together had given Gage the final reason he needed to end the marriage.

Turning off the lights, he walked downstairs, taking a good look around. A security guard stood outside, his eyes focused on the parking lot and driveway to the stockyards. He knew there'd be other men posted in the back and sides of the lot.

In a few days, there'd be another shipment of bucking stock arriving from Mexico. Gonzo would be there, as would the extra guards Ivan requested. Gage trusted his people, didn't believe any of them would be involved in something that could bring down Double Ace.

Then he thought of Brent. He'd trusted him, too. Perhaps he wasn't as good a judge of character as he always believed.

Chapter Ten

Crooked Tree

"Welcome back, Sam." Kade hugged his youngest sister, careful of the cast on her left arm. "You sure you're ready to get back to this madhouse?"

Sam grinned, looking at the front desk, which had become her home away from home after college. "More than ready. Sitting around the house is driving me crazy. Hope you have plenty of stuff for me to do. If not, I'll have to invent more work."

Kade stepped back, holding up his hands. "Don't even think about concocting ways to keep busy. There's plenty for you to do. When you're settled, come up to my office and I'll go over the work I've been saving for you."

"Will do." Sam looked at the clean desk. It looked the same as she'd left it before her accident. No stacks of mail to be sorted. No documents to be filed or shredded. Sam knew Rhett had helped out during her recuperation, working inside instead of in the stockyards where he preferred. As always, everyone did what they had to in order to keep the business going.

Kade looked over his shoulder as he walked up the stairs. "I've got an appointment coming in at nine. Let me know when he arrives and I'll come down to get him."

Nodding, she shoved her purse into an empty drawer and sat down, turning on her computer. Sam already knew there wouldn't be much of a backlog. Her laptop enabled her to work anywhere. As the unofficial assistant to both Kade and Skye, she'd kept herself busy during her time off. She'd missed the interaction with other employees and the occasional client who came through Crooked Tree.

Unlike some companies where the receptionist desk sat empty, a symbol as opposed to an actual position, the bucking stock group had a good number of scheduled appointments and walk-ins each day.

Pulling open a drawer, she picked up a file labeled *Vet Position* and read through the applications. She knew her father and uncles were considering hiring a company veterinarian who'd live in Fire Mountain, traveling to the other divisions on a regular basis. Kade and Skye had been interviewing candidates for the last two weeks. The night before, they'd taken one to dinner, and from what Skye told her, they were quite impressed. Matt and Cassie in Cold Creek and Mitch and Jace in Fire Mountain were doing the same. If the brothers decided to go ahead, the final selections would be interviewed at the company headquarters. Sam still didn't know if it was a good idea, but the brothers seemed determined to give it a try.

"Good morning, Sam."

Glancing up, her mouth dropped open. "Tucker. What are you doing here?"

He chuckled. "That's a heck of a welcome. I've been out of your house for a week and that's the best I get?"

Shaking her head, she stood and walked around the desk, giving him a hug. "Okay, so what *are* you doing here?" Returning to her desk, she looked at the computer.

"I have an appointment with Kade. Didn't he tell you?"

She spotted the appointment. "He mentioned a meeting this morning, but didn't mention you." Looking up, her eyes narrowed. "Is this about a job with us?"

"Nope. It's about a branding deal between your company and mine."

"Wow. A branding deal between MacLaren and Maverick? I think it's a great idea."

"Don't get too excited, Sam. I'm talking to several stock companies about it. Maverick could end up working with one of your competitors."

Sam shot him a look normally reserved for those she considered delusional. Tucker had been the object of it more than once. "You'll never find a better partner than my family. I don't know why you're even wasting your time with the others."

"That's why I'm here. To see what MacLaren has to offer."

Rolling her eyes, she hit the intercom. "Kade, Tuck...I mean, Mr. Kimball is here for your meeting." She thought she heard her brother chuckle.

"I'll be right down."

She looked at Tucker. "He'll—"

He nodded. "I heard." Crossing his arms, he let his gaze wander over her. "It must feel good to get back to work."

It hadn't taken him long to locate an apartment. He'd stayed at the house less than a week before moving into the one bedroom unit not far from Maverick headquarters. They'd spoken on the phone and texted a few times, but hadn't seen each other until today.

"I liked working from home. It's nice to be back around people, though. I'm thinking I wouldn't make a very good hermit."

He snorted. "Not hardly, Sam."

Kade came down the stairs, extending his hand. "Tucker. It's good to see you. How's the job going?"

Accepting the outstretched hand, he nodded. "Better than expected."

"Come on upstairs and you can tell me all about it."

Sam watched as Tucker followed Kade upstairs. She'd heard all kinds of comments about how well MacLaren men filled out their jeans. Her friends could build entire conversations around the subject. In her mind, no one looked better in them than Tucker Kimball.

Sighing, she sat down, staring at the computer screen. It had taken her a while to come to terms with the fact he'd never see her as anything more than a friend. When he'd broken up with his girlfriend, Sam had thought maybe he'd turn to her, figure out how she felt about him. Instead, he'd chosen someone else. The relationship didn't last long—just long enough for Sam to figure out he needed someone far different from her.

He might be single now, but if history held any clues, he'd soon have some tall, slim fashionista on his arm. As with his college girlfriends, the woman would be sophisticated and experienced. The sad truth was, his preferences were nothing like her.

A couple inches shorter than Skye's above average height, Sam had more curves than her older sister. Where people described Skye as beautiful or stunning, they'd label Sam as cute, pretty in a wholesome sort of way. She'd always wished she had her sister's long, sleek blonde hair. Instead, her dark auburn hair seemed to have a mind of its own. She usually wrestled it into a braid that fell down her back. Today, it fell over her shoulder. It may not be the most fashionable style, but it kept her long tresses out of her face, which was all she really required.

Shaking off the mood that had shifted from eager to downright surly, Sam forced herself to deal with real life, not the one she'd fantasized about for far too long.

Houston

"Sounds good, Tucker. I look forward to seeing you in Cold Creek next week."

Gage hung up, more than a little surprised at the conversation. Unlike some consumer product executives he'd dealt with, Tucker didn't pull any punches, preferring to get everything out so the decision makers could come up with the right solution. Upfront, honest, and willing to compromise to make a good opportunity work. They were traits he'd heard

Maverick looked for in their people, and they seemed to have found it in Tucker.

Kade had already set up a follow-up meeting in Cold Creek to discuss the additional rodeo contracts. It now appeared they'd also be talking about a branding proposal encompassing Maverick, Double Ace, and MacLaren. An unusual concept to be sure. Then again, Maverick always seemed to be at the forefront of marketing innovations.

"Gage."

He hit the intercom. "Yes, Daria."

"Mr. Santiago called. He said he tried to get through to you direct. I hope it was all right, but I told him you were on a call with Kade." Daria had been more hesitant around Gage since their discussion, as if she weren't quite sure of herself anymore.

"No problem. Did Ivan say what he wanted?"

"He needs to speak with you right away. Told me it's critical. He asked for you to use his private number."

"Thanks."

He pulled out his phone, calling the number Ivan had given him during his last visit. It rang once before he picked up.

"Gage, hold on a minute. I need to go somewhere private."

He couldn't tell anything from Ivan's tone. The fact he wanted to talk on the private line gave the only clue it might be a serious situation.

"Are you alone in your office?" Ivan asked, the first signs of strain in his voice.

"Yes. I'm on my private phone. What's going on?"

"The situation here is serious, my friend. Mother and Aunt Reyna were taken hostage last night."

"What the hell?" Gage stood, pacing away from his desk to the window.

"The men who took them are those we spoke of last time. The women weren't harmed and were set free this morning. It was a warning, nothing more."

"A warning about what?" Gage couldn't imagine the fear Ivan must have felt the last twenty-four hours.

"My father is unsure of the exact message they're trying to send, but is certain it has to do with the stock business and shipments to the United States. He's meeting with my uncles this evening."

"You'll be in the meeting, right, Ivan?"

"Yes, my friend. I will." Ivan paused a moment before continuing. "My mother and Aunt Reyna are not safe here."

"What can I do to help?"

"Nothing yet. I don't know if they plan more, but I am now certain those who took the women are responsible for the raid in Houston. My mother and aunt are packing. Mother will be staying at a safe place in California. I need to call Kade, see if Reyna can stay with him."

Gage nodded, remembering Ivan's aunt Reyna was Kade's mother. "From what I know, he stays in a small apartment in Crooked Tree. Brooke flies up for weekends, or he flies down to Fire Mountain. Perhaps it would be better for your aunt to stay there. The property is more isolated, a good number of ranch hands scattered around."

"I've thought of that, but it is where Rafe lives. My aunt, well…she is reluctant to ask a favor of him or any of the MacLarens."

"Ivan, call Kade. Ask his advice."

The silence stretched on, then Ivan blew out a breath. "You are right. I will call Kade and try to convince my aunt to go to Fire Mountain. It will be the safest place for her."

"And your mother."

"Ah, you do not know her, Gage. She will go only if she has access to her shopping and extravagances. No. My mother will be happier staying where there are servants and drivers." Ivan's voice sobered. "Keep watch. I am certain the stockyards are part of whatever is going on, and the trucking company is involved. The men you hired…can they be trusted?"

Gage thought of the additional guards, their backgrounds, and who had provided their names. "Yes. I trust them completely."

"Then we've done all we can for now. I will be in touch soon."

"Ivan, wait. I have meetings in Cold Creek next week. Should I cancel?"

"No. Continue as if all is normal, but be watchful. I'll let you know if I learn more from my uncles."

Gage felt a ball of fear build in his stomach as Ivan hung up. He had no experience with the type of men who would kidnap women, smuggle drugs or other contraband, doing whatever necessary to protect their interests. His scariest moments were on the back of an angry horse. The current situation couldn't even compare.

He picked up the phone, making a call he should've made within days after the raid.

"Thad, it's Gage. Call me. We need to meet."

"I wish I had more for you, Gage. My sources aren't talking, other than to say they were aware of the Santiago kidnapping." Thad took another bite of his carne asada burrito, his eyes scanning the area. They sat outside a small restaurant.

"Do they know who was behind the abduction?"

"If they do, they're not saying." Thad washed down the food with a sip of his beer before digging into his chili rellenos. They didn't speak as a group of young men walked toward them, stopping a few feet away, speaking Spanish in hushed tones. When they moved on, Thad set down his fork, nodding behind him. "Those boys are part of a local street gang tied to the Serrano cartel."

"Never heard of it." Gage looked over Thad's shoulder at the boys disappearing down an alley.

"It's a small cartel, looking to grow by any means possible. They're into drugs, extortion, trafficking."

"Of young girls?" Gage's jaw hardened at the thought.

"Boys," Thad sneered. "Old man Serrano's men will deal in girls, too, but his clients prefer boys. It's a sick business."

Gage shook his head, disgust twisting his features. "Do you think they could be involved in the Santiago kidnapping?"

"Not unless they're one of the cartels doing business with Ivan's uncles. I think it was one of the larger cartels in central Mexico. My guess is either the Montalvo-Ortiz cartel or the de la Garza cartel. They have ties with the Santiago family going way back."

"You know that from your sources?" Gage set down the remainder of his burrito.

"Nope. From my days with the DEA." Sliding his empty plate aside, Thad rested his arms on the table. "Both are manic in their quest for power and enlarging their territories. Unless things have changed, both traffic drugs. I have heard both have business arrangements with the Santiago brothers."

"Including Javier, Ivan's father?"

"I don't have specifics, Gage. What you need to know is how unstable the situation is around León, where the Santiagos make their home. My sense is the uneasy truce between the families is ending. I also suspect Javier's brothers are into more than he knows or admits to Ivan." He leaned closer to Gage, his voice lowering further. "Ivan needs to get his mother, aunt, and anyone else he cares about out of León." Sitting back, he crossed his arms.

"We've already spoken about getting his mother and aunt out. Tell me. What are your thoughts on Eddie Gonzalez?"

"Your stock manager?"

Gage nodded. "It seems you have concerns about him."

"It may not be Gonzalez, but someone with a certain level of credibility inside Double Ace is feeding the feds false information."

Gage rubbed his chin. "What would they have to gain if the feds perform a raid and find nothing?"

"It pulls attention away from what's really going on, focusing on your operations. The independent trucking firm is the key. Someone at your company is working for them."

"We've checked each shipment, searched the trucks. We came up empty. From what Gonzo found, all they're shipping is cattle."

"I'd bet my meager government retirement they're bringing more than cattle across the border. Without a professional crew to tear the trucks apart, it's doubtful you'll find anything. You'll need to focus on finding the employee working for the truckers. Whoever they are, they have the feds' attention, which doesn't bode well for you." Pulling out some money, he tossed it on the table. "I've got to take off. I'll be in touch as soon as I have more."

Gage watched him leave, feeling as if he'd stepped into another world. All he wanted to do was supply bucking stock to his rodeo clients, keeping connected to the sport he loved. Instead, those in charge of the company he worked for might be involved in activities that put him, his employees, and his customers in danger. Thad's implied warning stuck with him. He needed to discover the person or persons at Double Ace providing information to the feds. Once he did, they'd have their connection to the trucking company, and possibly the cartel.

Chapter Eleven

Fire Mountain
MacLaren Enterprises Headquarters

"Heath, do you have a minute?"

"Whatever amount of time you need, Rafe." Heath closed his laptop. "Have a seat." He glanced up, seeing the lines of worry on his brother's face. "What's wrong?"

"I don't know all the details, but Kade called. He heard from his cousin, Ivan Santiago. His mother and aunt were abducted."

Heath leaned forward. "You're talking about Kade's mother?"

Rafe nodded. "Reyna and her sister-in-law. They were released within hours. Ivan and his family believe it was a warning of some kind. They've requested our help."

"Anything, you know that."

"They have a place in California where Ivan's mother can stay. It's guarded and somewhat secluded." Rafe rubbed the back of his neck.

"And Reyna?"

"Kade asked if she could come here. Stay on the ranch until things calm down."

Heath's brow lifted. "You know you don't have to ask me if it's all right. She's welcome to stay as long as needed."

Rafe glanced away, focusing on the mountains visible through Heath's window.

"You don't want her here?"

He didn't turn to look at his brother. "It isn't that. I want her safe, and this is the best place."

Heath sat back in his chair and waited. Unlike him and their younger brother, Jace, Rafe could be impatient, spurred into action with scant information. The contemplative, quiet side of him wasn't something Heath saw often.

"Reyna should stay at the big house with you and Annie."

"You'll be all right with her in the same house as you?" It had been obvious to Heath, and most of the rest of the family celebrating Cassie and Matt's wedding, that Rafe and Reyna still cared about each other, had unfinished business they needed to settle.

"I'll move into one of the family cabins."

The MacLarens owned several cabins not far from the main house, each furnished and having two bedrooms, a bath, and full kitchen. Kade and Brooke stay in one when they were in town, and Ernesto Salgado moved into another when Heath hired him to head up security. Several sat empty.

"There's no need for you to move. The ranch house has plenty of space and several empty bedrooms with private baths. Besides, it isn't as if you need a chaperone." The amusement in Heath's voice got Rafe's attention.

Rafe slapped his hands on the desk and stood. "Hell if I know what we need." He sucked in a breath, pacing a few steps away. "The woman drives me crazy, has since the first time I saw her."

"If you're still in love with Reyna, you should tell her."

Rafe turned toward Heath, crossing his arms, his features hard. "Why? So she can run off again, like she did when we were younger?"

Heath held up his hands, palms out. "Hey, this is between the two of you. I'm just saying if she stays here, whether you're in the house or a cabin, you'll see each other. Maybe it's time to get it all out in the open."

Rafe dropped his arms, his shoulders drooping enough for Heath to see. "Ever since the wedding, I can't get her off my mind. I never thought I'd see her again, then…" A heavy sigh escaped as he lowered himself back into the chair.

"Would it be so bad if you two got back together?"

Rafe snorted. "Trust me. There's no chance of that happening. Her brother, Javier, hates me, and I'm not so certain Reyna doesn't feel the same. The issue now is keeping her safe. I feel better with Nesto on board and living at the ranch." He glanced at Heath. "We may need to hire a couple more men."

"Hire however many you need."

Rafe blew out a breath, then stood. "I'll call Ivan and tell him she's welcome here."

"And you'll stay in the house?"

Walking to the door, he nodded. "For now. Just be sure to keep one of the cabins empty."

Cold Creek

Skye couldn't seem to settle down. Within an hour, Gage would arrive from Houston. Matt had told her he planned to be available for two days, then stay the weekend. As usual, those from out of town would stay at the same hotel.

Cassie had invited her and everyone else—Kade, Nesto, Janie, Gage, and Brooke, who planned to fly in Friday—to dinner at their place that night. Kade, Brooke, and Nesto would head back to Fire Mountain on Sunday, arriving in time to meet Reyna at the airport. Skye didn't fly out until early Monday morning, the same as Gage.

"Hey, Skye. Do you have time to go over the final agreements for the additional rodeos before Gage arrives?"

She glanced up from the desk in the cubicle Matt provided. "Sure, Cassie. Anything to keep me busy."

"Didn't bring along enough work, huh?"

She shrugged. No one except Kade knew about her and Gage, and she planned to keep it that way. "I figured we'd be in meetings most of today, so I left several files at the hotel. I'll bring them tomorrow. You know, so I have stuff to keep me busy if the meetings end early…" Skye cringed at the way she rambled.

Cassie leaned against the cubicle divider, trying to hide a smile. "Are you okay?"

"Yeah, fine. Grab a chair from next door and let's go over the agreements."

"Here you two are." Janie stood in the hall, her arms loaded with binders. "Matt asked everyone to meet in the conference room."

"Did Nesto and Gage arrive?" Cassie stood, picking up the agreements.

"Yep. Everyone's here. Coffee's all set up, and the receptionist brought snacks to tide you over until lunch."

"You'll be in the meetings, right, Janie?" Skye liked Janie, and still couldn't reconcile the fact Kurt wanted nothing to do with her.

Standing, Skye followed them toward the conference room, her stomach in knots. She thought there'd been time for her to get over Gage calling it off. After all, their time together had been brief, certainly nothing to warrant the dread building inside her.

"Today for sure. Matt wants me to hear what Nesto has to say about new security measures and take notes when we talk about the agreements with Double Ace. I don't know about tomorrow." Janie opened the door, letting Cassie and Skye pass before following them in.

Everyone else already had seats. Janie quickly took her place between Kade and Nesto. Skye looked at the others, noticing one empty chair between Gage and Nesto, another next to Matt. She started toward it, hesitating when Cassie moved in the same direction. Resigned, she took the chair next to Gage, scooting as far away from him as possible without drawing attention. She shifted toward Nesto, her back to Gage.

"Good morning, Skye." She could feel the warmth of his breath on her neck and straightened. Glancing over her shoulder, she frowned, noticing he'd moved his chair a little closer.

"Hello, Gage. I hope you had a good trip." Her words were clipped, professional.

"As good as you'd expect."

Matt cleared his throat. "Good morning. I'm going to handle the morning session, while Kade takes over in the afternoon. I believe you all know Ernesto Salgado, our new head of security." They all nodded, smiling at Nesto. "He's going to go over his thoughts on security and recommendations. I hope you don't find this too boring, Gage. Kade and I thought you might have questions since some of Nesto's recommendations impact our clients."

"No problem, Matt. I'd like to hear what he says. We may want to include some of his suggestions at Double Ace."

"All right, Nesto. Why don't you start?"

Two hours later, after discussing in detail each recommendation and how to implement it, they wrapped up. Most were simple enough. Other suggestions would take time and the installation of new equipment, which had already been approved by the brothers.

Gage needed a break and a cold shower. Being inches away from Skye for so long tested his sanity and control to the point of breaking. He'd traveled up here knowing how difficult it would be, surprised it was worse than anticipated. His limits were tested every time she spoke. The familiar vanilla and coconut scent had his body on edge every minute.

"Let's take a break while Janie gets lunch set up." Matt's announcement had them all standing, stretching, and moving toward the door. "Gage, wait up."

He turned, almost knocking Skye over. "Sorry."

Shrugging, she moved past him, as if she couldn't get away fast enough.

"Cassie and I are going out tonight. Why don't you join us?"

Gage watched Skye walk down the hall. A sense of longing so great it felt like a physical blow caught him off guard. "Uh, sure. If I won't be in the way."

Matt clasped him on the shoulder. "Not a chance. It'll be good to catch up. You're still coming over Saturday, right?"

Gage nodded, still trying to wrap his mind around the realization his feelings for Skye might be more than a passing case of lust. He'd gained a new respect for her as he listened to the thoughtful questions she asked Nesto, the way she brought up suggestions. Her intelligence and humor had always attracted him. Her passion in bed stunned him. No woman had ever been so open, so honest in her lovemaking. Her unrestrained response and giving nature couldn't compare to anything he'd ever experienced.

Gage continued watching her as she spoke with Janie and Cassie. Agitation and regret washed over him. He wanted to slam his hand against the wall, knowing he'd been the one to turn away, end something just beginning to take shape.

"Gage?" Matt followed the direction of his gaze, his brows furrowing.

"Huh? Oh, sorry, man. Yes, I'll definitely be there on Saturday."

"You aren't thinking about starting something with Skye, are you?"

Gage turned to glare at his friend. He had it with those close to Skye warning him off, even if they were well-intentioned.

"And what if I am?"

Matt didn't flinch under Gage's hard stare. Instead, he nodded toward his office. "Follow me."

Gage shook his head, keeping his mouth shut.

Once in the office, Matt closed the door, rounding on Gage. "Are you already seeing her?"

"What *is* it with you MacLarens?" Gage ground out, pacing toward the window. "First Kade, now you."

"First, I'm a Garner, not a MacLaren. Second…is there already something going on?"

Gage let out a deep breath. This was not why he came to Cold Creek. He didn't discuss his emotions or talk about the women he dated. Not ever. He'd make an exception this one time.

"Something *was* going on until I made the mistake of letting Kade's warning sway me. I'm determined to set things right with Skye and start seeing her again."

Matt let out a whispered string of curses. "Geez, Gage. A man with your track record can't just walk in and start messing around with someone like Skye. She's not like your other women. Not even close."

Gage walked to within a foot of him, planting his feet. "Let me be clear, Matt. What I feel or don't feel for Skye isn't any of your business." When Matt started to speak, he held up his hand. "But I know you're doing this because you're concerned about her. And I know you have every right to have reservations about me." Turning, Gage walked a few feet away, wanting to get control before saying something he'd later regret. When he spoke, his voice was calm, determined. "It's different with Skye. I can't get her out of my head. The damn woman is there when I wake up and when I fall asleep. There are days I feel as if I'm losing my mind."

"Wow," Matt breathed out, unable to fathom the change in his friend.

"Yeah. Wow." Gage pinched the bridge of his nose, then crossed his arms, staring outside.

For a minute, neither spoke, then Matt broke the silence. "Is this how you felt about Gwen?"

Gage swung around to face his friend. "Not even close." Dropping his arms to his sides, he walked over to the small sofa and lowered himself onto it. "I know it isn't smart to get involved with her. It's the main reason I called it off a couple weeks ago. The thing is, I can't seem to let it go." He stared at Matt. "I don't *want* to let her go."

"But she's hurt and pissed," Matt guessed, but it made sense. He knew something had been going on with Skye. He just hadn't known what.

"And she'll barely say two words to me. Although they are civil." He tried to smile, but it didn't reach his eyes.

"Well, the way I see it, you have about three days, maybe four to get her to listen. But I warn you, friend or not, if you screw with her, I won't have a choice but to come after you."

"Yeah. You, Kade, Mitch, Sean, Rhett, probably Rafe, and God knows who else. Well, you all know where to find me." Pushing himself up, Gage walked to the door, resting his hand on the knob. "I can't make promises. If she does agree to see me again, I can't guarantee it will work out. All I can say is I'm not messing around here. Do you get me on this?"

Matt nodded. "Yeah, man. I get you."

By the end of the day, Gage still hadn't gotten Skye to say more than a few words to him. When the group discussed the partnership with Double Ace, she commented on clauses in the agreement, always keeping her voice calm and professional. By the time Kade called it a day, Gage still didn't have a clue about how to make things right with her.

Matt walked up as the room cleared. "Cassie's in a separate car. Why don't you follow me to the restaurant?"

"Works for me." Gage stepped into the hall, hoping Skye might still be hanging around. "I'll meet you up front, Matt. I've got a couple calls to make, so take your time."

"Good meeting, Gage." He turned to see Janie coming up behind him, a load of files in one arm, purse in the other.

"Will you be in the meetings tomorrow?"

"Maybe in the afternoon." Janie slid her purse over her shoulder, shifting the files to her other arm. "Kade asked me to give Nesto a tour of the place, then take him to meet a couple vendors. One is the firm that installed the security system a couple years ago."

"Nesto seems the perfect person to head security."

"I guess he and Kade have known each other since they were teens. According to Matt, the brothers were all behind the hire."

"The brothers?" Gage cocked his head to the side.

She smiled. "Heath, Rafe, and Jace."

"You ready?" Matt joined them. "Cassie is already on her way."

"Still need to make a couple calls, but I can do that at the restaurant."

"I'll see you two tomorrow." Janie walked to the door Gage held open for her, all of them heading to their cars.

"I'm in the black sports car."

"Figures," Matt called over his shoulder as Gage headed in the opposite direction.

Five minutes later, they pulled into the parking lot of an Italian restaurant Gage hadn't noticed before. The nondescript single-story building sat back from the street. A red awning with *Guido's* in big white letters set off the entrance.

"The best Italian food west of Denver." Matt walked up next to him.

"I'm guessing west of Denver and east of Utah."

"You got me there." Matt laughed, slipping his keys into his pocket.

Gage hit the button to lock the car, following Matt to the entrance. "Seriously, if they have a good wine selection, I'm fine with however the food comes out."

"Why do you think I come here? Plus, they have an incredible selection of single malt scotch." Matt pushed the door open, motioning for Gage to go first. Greeting the hostess, they followed her to a table in a back corner.

Gage looked around, letting his eyes adjust to the dark interior. The place was real old-school with dark paneled wood walls, red leather booths lining them, and tables in the center. Beautiful oil paintings, most of landscapes, adorned the walls. Shifting his gaze, he stopped. At the corner booth sat Cassie, Skye next to her. Matt turned abruptly, his face a mask.

"I had no idea, man."

Gage shook his head. "Don't worry about it. This might even work to my advantage." That was what he told himself until he saw the look of horror on Skye's face. As he got to the booth, she started to stand, her hand gripping her purse. "You're not thinking of running out, are you, Skye?"

He could almost see the wheels in her mind turn before she sighed and sat back down.

"Of course not."

"Good." Gage didn't wait another instant as he slid in next to her.

Cassie looked at Skye, then Gage, before returning to stare at Skye. "Is there something I need to know?"

"No," Skye and Gage said at the same time, Gage sending a warning look to Matt, who did his best to wipe the smile from his face.

"Okay…" Cassie picked up her menu, scanning it quickly, then laying it down.

When the waitress came by, Gage and Skye ordered whiskey, Matt a scotch, and Cassie a large iced tea.

"Tea? Are you all right, Cass?" Skye scooted closer to her, providing a little distance between her and Gage.

Cassie glanced at Matt, covering his hand with hers. "I'm great. Just don't feel like drinking is all."

"What do you recommend?" Gage set his menu aside, pretty certain he'd go for the osso buco.

"Matt usually gets the lasagna, sometimes the osso buco. I like the angel hair pasta with pesto. The chicken piccata is also good."

"The chicken piccata sounds, um…perfect." Skye's voice faltered when Gage's thigh moved against hers.

It took less than a minute to place their orders, all the while Skye searching for a way to get some distance between herself and Gage without alerting Cassie and Matt. She didn't know what he was doing, except trying to bait her. Without question, she knew sitting next to him all evening wasn't going to work, not with his leg rubbing against hers, their shoulders brushing against each other every few minutes.

Cassie's phone rang. "Oh, sorry." She glanced at the screen. "I'd better take this, then I promise to put it away." Matt stood, allowing her to get out.

"I'll be right back." Matt walked away, leaving Skye and Gage alone.

"What are you doing?" Skye hissed.

Gage picked up a piece of bread, breaking off a piece. "I don't know what you mean."

"Of course you do. Stop rubbing your leg against me."

"You always liked it before. In fact, you—"

She put a hand over his mouth. "Don't even think about going there."

Gage chuckled. "Darlin', I think about going there all the time. With you." He winked, popping a piece of bread into his mouth.

"Look, Gage. I don't know what game you're playing, but I'm really not up for it. *You're* the one who called it off."

Chewing slowly, he swallowed, then washed the bread down with his whiskey. "Maybe I made a mistake."

Her eyes widened, then sparked in anger. "A mistake?"

"Shhh, sweetheart. You don't want the whole restaurant to hear you."

Grinding her teeth, Skye continued to glare at him. "You said you didn't want to see me anymore."

"No. I said it probably wasn't *smart* for us to see each other. I never said I didn't *want* to see you." He picked up her glass, tipping it to her lips. "Take a sip. It might calm you down."

She almost growled in anger, then snatched the glass out of his hand, swallowing half the contents.

Sobering, Gage let his hand rest on her leg, pleased when she didn't push it away. "After dinner, come to my room. Or I'll come to yours. We'll talk, figure something out."

Shaking her head, she downed the rest of the whiskey. "No."

"Then we'll go someplace else. Wherever you want. Give me a few minutes to set things right between us."

Signaling the waitress, she held up her glass.

"Getting drunk isn't going to help, Skye."

She shot him a contemptuous glare. "How do you know what will help and what won't?" The gleam in his eyes told her she'd gone in the wrong direction. "Forget that." Picking up the fresh drink, she took a small sip, then sat back. "It's over, Gage. Why can't you leave it alone?"

The misery on her face almost had him backing away. "Is that what you honestly want? For me to ignore how I feel about you?"

Her lips parted. "What do you mean?"

When Gage saw Matt and Cassie approaching, he lowered his voice. "Give me some time after dinner. I'll do my best to explain."

She nodded, although not at all sure what she'd be getting herself into.

Chapter Twelve

"I'll drop you off at the hotel on my way home." Cassie walked into the parking lot with Skye. "It'll give us a chance to talk."

"We're staying at the same place. She's welcome to ride with me." Gage stepped next to Skye, hoping she hadn't changed her mind. Seeing her body sway, he grabbed her arm.

Glancing between the two, Skye turned toward Cassie, her head swimming from one too many whiskeys. "There's no sense in you going out of your way. I'll ride with Gage."

"If you're sure." Cassie pulled out her keys, studying her cousin. "You might want to stop for coffee, Gage. Skye looks like she could use it."

"Hey, I'm standing right here." Skye shrugged off Gage's hold, crossing her arms.

Cassie rolled her eyes. "You may want to take a couple aspirin before going to bed."

Skye leaned into Gage, ignoring Cassie's suggestion. "I'll see you in the morning." Slipping her arm through his, she let him lead her to his car, waiting as he opened the door. "Can we stop somewhere? Cassie's right. I need some coffee."

Gage chuckled. "We can do that." Once she'd downed three whiskeys, he'd decided talking wasn't going to happen tonight. At least he'd made some progress. She'd agreed to let him take her to the hotel.

He drove in silence, glancing at her a few times to make sure she hadn't nodded off. As they turned into the hotel parking lot, she looked at him, cocking her head in question.

"There's a coffee shop next door. Seemed the best place to stop."

Gage took hold of her hand as he helped her out, tucking it through his arm again. "I counted three whiskeys. Did I miss one?"

Skye shrugged. "I don't know. Maybe one before you and Matt showed up."

"I hope you didn't power them down because of me."

She tried to pull away, but he tightened his hold as he grabbed the door. "Of course not."

"Take any seat." The waitress didn't look up from where she took another customer's money.

Choosing a booth by the window, Gage let her pick a spot, then slid in next to her.

"There's room on the other side."

Gage grabbed the menus, handing one to her. "I'd rather sit next to you."

When the waitress walked up, Skye looked at the menu, shaking her head. "Just coffee."

"Same for me."

Skye crossed her arms, scooting closer to the window, turning slightly so she faced him. "What did you want to talk about?"

Gage didn't want to do this when she'd had too much to drink. "It might be best to wait until tomorrow."

"I'm not drunk."

"I realize you're not. I'm thinking it might be better to wait until both of us have clear heads."

She snorted, rolling her eyes. "Look. We're here. I'm ready to listen to what you have to say."

Gage waited as the waitress set down their coffees and a bowl with containers of cream. "Let me know if you want anything else."

Skye poured cream into her cup, adding a packet of sweetener, then settled back in the booth and waited. Gage took a sip, then shifted toward her.

"We had plans the last time we met. They got messed up when I received an urgent message from work. Trust me, Skye. It was important and had to be dealt with right away."

Her features softened. "Can you tell me what it was about?"

"Not yet, but it won't affect our partnership." He held his cup with both hands, feeling the warmth seep into his skin. "I suspect you thought the text I sent was meant to break off what we had going. It wasn't."

Her brows scrunched together. "On the phone, you said…" She rubbed a hand across her brow to clear her head.

"I said our seeing each other might not be smart."

"Right."

"It's still not smart, but damned if I'm going to back off because I'm uncertain."

Taking a slow sip of coffee, Skye tried to relax and let her alcohol clouded brain sort out what he said. "I don't know what you want. You're going to have to be more clear."

He held out his cup, letting the waitress top it off. "Look. My marriage was a joke that didn't end well. It's been over four years and I finally got all ties cut just about the time you and I first met. The last thing I want is to get tied to anyone."

She nodded. "I know. You've been quite clear. It's why we agreed to no strings, keeping it casual."

Gage cleared his throat. "Yeah, about that. It seems I'm finding it harder than I thought to keep things light with you. What's best for me is to not get tangled up in a relationship where someone could get hurt. Do you understand?"

She began to nod, then shook her head. "I guess not."

"Let me try this." He turned to face her completely, his voice low and sincere. "I don't do more than one night with a woman. Haven't since Gwen and I split up. We've been together a couple times and I already know it isn't enough. I like you. Much more than I anticipated, which isn't what I'd planned."

He saw the corners of her mouth tilt up, wishing she'd send him one of her bright smiles.

"So, what do you want to do?" She nodded when the waitress passed again, holding up the pot of coffee. Adding cream and sweetener, she looked at him, holding his gaze.

"I wish I knew. You have to understand, I'm not a good bet. My head is still messed up from the circumstances around the divorce."

"Seems we both have trust issues. Did I tell you I walked in on my fiancé with one of my close friends?"

His nostrils flared as anger spread through him. "Shit. No, you never mentioned it."

"It's probably why I hardly date, never let things go too far. With you, though…" She sucked in a breath. "I guess you're just too hard to resist."

He stared at her a long time before responding. "I walked in on my brother and my wife."

She nearly jumped out of her seat as her eyes widened. "My God, Gage. That must've been awful." Shaking her head, she thought of what she might have done under the same circumstances. "Do you still talk to him?"

"No." His voice had gone cold, distant, as if he'd been transported back in time. "I told him to get out. That's the last I saw of either one of them until Gwen and I met to finalize the money part of our divorce."

She blew out a breath. "Geez. I can't even imagine."

He downed the last of his coffee, setting the cup aside. "If someone had told me an hour before what I'd see when I walked in on them, I'd have told them they were nuts. My brother and I were close. I didn't trust anyone more than him." He looked up, his eyes full of pain. "Seems I'm not a very good judge of people."

Skye didn't know what to say. Her experience had hurt. Gage's story went well beyond the incident with her fiancé.

"My head still isn't on straight when it comes to women." He reached over, taking one of her hands in his. "I don't know how much I have to offer. It's important to me you don't get hurt, Skye."

Placing her other hand on top of his, she squeezed. "I never asked you for a guarantee."

Shaking his head slowly, he watched her expression change from deep compassion to intense yearning. "No, you didn't. You've never asked for anything."

"Except honesty, Gage. If you still want to give us a try, all I'll ask is for you to be honest. I don't do well with lies."

Nodding, he wrapped an arm around her shoulders, placing a kiss on her forehead. "I don't know anyone who does." Looking at her empty coffee cup, he slid out of the booth and stood, holding out his hand. "Let's get back to the hotel. We have an early day tomorrow."

A loud pounding on her door had Skye sitting up, groaning, holding her head with both hands.

"Skye. Wake up. It's time to leave for the office."

Gage?

The pounding started again when she didn't respond.

"I'm up," she ground out, wincing as she rolled out of bed and padded to the door. Pulling it open, she didn't hesitate to grab the cup of coffee Gage held out. Turning, she didn't say another word as she disappeared into the bathroom.

"What, no morning kiss?"

"Later," she called, her voice hoarse as she closed the door behind her.

Gage chuckled as he settled into an overstuffed chair. The sound of the shower and an occasional groan could be heard through the bathroom door as he scanned a copy of the national newspaper he'd picked up outside her door.

When they'd returned from the coffee shop the night before, she'd invited him to stay. Refusing her hadn't been easy. Skye had made it plain she disagreed with his decision to tuck her in with a couple kisses, then leave.

Staying wasn't smart. Gage didn't want to see confusion or regret on her face if she woke to see him sharing her bed. When they made love the next time, both would be certain of what was happening.

Another loud groan drew his attention away from the night before to the newspaper in his hand. A few minutes later, Skye shoved the door open, steam flowing out of the bathroom.

Gage didn't look up from the story he read about renewed violence in Mexico. "Take a couple aspirin."

Skimming the story, he focused on the part about drug wars in the central part of the country. There had been an uptick in kidnappings and murder. Standing, he pulled his phone from his pocket, then punched in a number. Walking to the other side of the room, he kept his back to the bathroom.

"Ivan, it's Gage. I'll be in Cold Creek until Monday. Checking on the status in León. If you need help, anything at all, let me know." Turning, he saw Skye, still wrapped in a towel, standing a few feet away.

"León. That's where Kade's mother lives, right?"

"Yes."

He walked up to her and placed his hands on her shoulders, drawing her in for a kiss. The instant his mouth touched hers, his body responded. Her hands inched up his arms, circling his neck, urging him to deepen the kiss.

One hand roamed her back while the other moved to the knot in front where she'd secured the towel. One tug and the knot gave way, dropping to pool at her feet. Groaning, he lifted her into his arms, carrying her to the bed. Laying her down, Gage let his gaze wander over her, his heart beating so hard as to be almost painful.

"You are so beautiful." His deep, uneven voice washed over her as his hand moved along her calf, up her thigh, and over a hip, resting on her waist.

"You know, this doesn't work as well when one of us still has clothes on."

Mumbling a curse, he drew the back of his hand down her cheek. "We don't have time."

"There's enough."

"No, Skye, there isn't. But I'll take what I can get." Lowering his mouth to hers, he claimed her with a frantic intensity new to him.

Shifting, he let her hands come between them, her fingers making fast work of the buttons on his shirt before freeing the button on his jeans, pulling down the zipper.

"Are you sure, Skye? This won't be soft or slow."

Skye smiled up at him. "I don't care. All I want is you."

"Let's give them another five minutes, then we'll start." Kade had already tried calling both Skye and Gage, getting voicemail each time. Matt and Cassie had done the same.

Skye dashed through the door, not meeting anyone's eyes as she took a seat. "Sorry. We, um…got held up."

Gage met Kade's stare, then Matt's, holding them until he took a seat next to Skye. He could see Janie biting her lower lip, Cassie's amused gaze cutting to Skye, then Matt.

"Do either of you want coffee?" Cassie asked, getting ready to stand.

"No. We're good." Gage answered for both of them, then winced at the mistake.

Kade shuffled some papers, rubbing his brow, giving them time to settle in. "If we're all ready, we need to talk about a family situation before moving on to other business."

"Do you want me to step out?"

"No, Gage. This concerns you, too."

Gage could feel Skye's eyes on him. Glancing at her, he could see the question on her face.

"My mother, Reyna Santiago, and Ivan's mother were kidnapped a few days ago, held hostage for a few hours, then released."

Cassie's hand flew to her mouth. Janie gasped, as did Skye.

"My God, Kade. Are they all right?" Skye looked over at Gage, remembering the call she'd overheard earlier that morning.

"They're fine, Skye. Neither were harmed, but the message was clear. It is thought one or more of the cartels is waging war, the Santiago family in the crosshairs. Gage, through conversations with Ivan, and Nesto, as head of security, is already aware of what happened. There is no reason to believe anyone in the MacLaren family is being targeted. It appears the threats are directed at Ivan's father and uncles."

"What do you want us to do?" Cassie felt Matt's hand settle over hers.

"Nothing yet. The brothers have extended an offer for my mother to stay at the ranch in Fire Mountain as long as needed. She'll be arriving on Sunday. Brooke, Nesto, and I will meet her at the airport and escort her to the house. Ivan's mother is staying with her relatives somewhere in California." Kade took a breath, then looked up. "No one knows if anyone in the MacLaren family is being targeted, although it is doubtful. It seems to be an isolated war in central Mexico. Having my mother here is a precaution."

"It's the least we can do." Skye sat forward in her chair, resting her arms on the table. "Did whoever take them send a message or have any demands?"

"Nothing. It's not the typical abduction. At least not what I was used to seeing with the DEA." Standing, he pointed to a map on the wall of the United States and Mexico. "This is León, where Ivan's family lives. My mother lives with them. The house is fortified with security, bodyguards for each family member, and the women don't go anywhere without Ivan's father knowing where and when they'll return home."

Nesto stood, joining Kade. "In reviewing all the information available, talking to my contacts and Kade's, there is little doubt someone inside the Santiago household was involved. The family is working with the police in León, but as is common in Mexico, loyalties are few and a good number of the authorities are on the cartel payroll."

"Which cartels?" Gage studied the map, which also showed territories for various cartels and routes used for smuggling. He'd never seen a map like it.

Kade looked over his shoulder at the map, pointing to two names. "My guess is either the de la Garza cartel or possibly the Montalvo-Ortiz cartel."

The same ones Thad mentioned, Gage thought, wondering if his friend had learned anything more.

"Both use the borders of Texas, New Mexico, and Arizona to bring product into the country." Kade glanced around the table. "From what I know, both are moving beyond drugs. This is one reason the timing was perfect to bring Nesto on board. As you all know, our businesses run well beyond providing rodeo stock. We have real estate holdings in many western states, work with ranchers to help them increase profits, provide pleasure riding stock to buyers throughout the world, run a camp for foster children and a dude ranch for city people. My guess is the brothers aren't out of ideas. In short, we shouldn't believe we can never be a target. Anyone who comes between the cartels and their money is in danger."

"I'm working with all divisions to be smart when it comes to security. Thanks to Kade's background, we're able to provide training not available at most companies." Nesto cleared his throat, not wanting to tackle the next subject, knowing it had to be discussed. "The brothers are talking about bodyguards."

Matt's gaze shot to Nesto's. "For them?"

Nesto crossed his arms. "For them and most family members."

A collective groan came from those around the table.

"No." Cassie shot to her feet. "I am not going to have someone follow me around. It's just overkill at this point."

"Cass, sit down." Matt grabbed her hand, tugging her back into her chair. "Nesto said they're *discussing* it. No decision has been made. Right, Nesto?"

"That's my understanding. Heath thought you all should know in case they decide to proceed."

Kade stepped forward. "This isn't meant to scare all of you. It's meant as a warning for everyone to be aware of what's happening around them at all times. From what we can tell, we're all safe. We want to keep it that way."

Chapter Thirteen

"Anyone need directions to our place?" Cassie rushed to gather her files. She'd planned to leave a little early to stop by the grocery store and start dinner preparations for the crowd she and Matt had invited. As often happened, the meeting took longer than anticipated.

Gage looked at Skye. "You know how to get there, right?"

If it weren't for the serious topics they discussed, it would've been an agonizing day. He sat no more than a few inches away without the right to reach over and touch her, thread his fingers through hers. Gage couldn't remember ever wanting to connect with a woman physically the way he did Skye. Something about a simple touch cleared his head, giving him a sense of peace.

"Are you asking me to ride with you?" Her eyes danced in amusement.

He leaned down, lowering his voice. "I'm asking for more than that, but I'll settle for driving you to Cassie's."

She touched her cheek, feeling it heat. "And back to the hotel later, I hope."

"You can count on that."

"Are you guys ready to leave?" They turned to see Janie standing by the door, her hand on the light switch. Neither had realized they were the last two in the room.

Nodding, biting her lip to hold back a laugh, Skye grabbed her computer case and purse. "We'll see you at Cassie's, right?"

Janie shrugged. "I'm not sure. It's been a long week."

"I'm not letting you use some lame excuse not to show up. You have to eat, and it might as well be where you don't have to fix it." Skye walked alongside her, stepping outside as Gage held the door open for them. "At least come for a while, keep Nesto company. You know, he's going through some personal stuff, too."

Janie stopped, tilting her head. "What do you mean?"

"I probably shouldn't say much, but he and his long-time girlfriend split a few months ago. From what Kade said, he's doing all right, but not great. I think leaving the U.S. Marshal Service and coming to work for us has been good for him."

Janie shook her head. "He's such a great guy. I can't imagine letting someone like him go. Guess you never know what's going on in someone else's mind."

They both knew she didn't refer just to Nesto and his girlfriend. Everyone thought they knew her fiancé, Kurt, and how deep his love for Janie was. His injuries from the fire had twisted something inside him, hardening him, even to Janie's love.

"Guess not." Skye touched her arm. "We'll see you there?"

"At least for a while." Janie climbed into the vintage sports car she treated as if it were her child, and drove off.

"Nice car." Gage looked around. Seeing no one, he settled his arm over Skye's shoulders.

"After college, her parents gave her money to buy whatever car she wanted. Of all the choices, she picked a sleek, older sports car she'd been dreaming of for a long time." She leaned into him as they approached his car.

Turning her to him, he leaned down. The kiss started as a quick brush of the lips, then heated until he had to force himself to step away.

"I don't know what the hell you do to me, Skye."

She could say the same about him. "Is that a good thing?"

Opening the door, letting her get in, he nodded. "I'd say it is."

Truthfully, Gage didn't know if it was good or bad. He'd go along for the ride, though, giving himself time to figure it out. At some point, he felt certain the newness would wear off and they'd drift apart, or one of them would meet someone else. For now, he'd take it all in and enjoy himself.

They didn't stop at the hotel to change. Skye wanted to pick up some wine, and Gage planned to buy a bottle of scotch for Matt. He'd forgotten how much his friend enjoyed a glass of single malt until he'd ordered it at the restaurant.

Skye had fretted all day over asking Gage the question poking at her. When they got back in the car, their purchases secure in the trunk, she couldn't wait any longer. "Do we say anything about us, or keep it to ourselves?"

Gage kept his eyes straight ahead, the muscle in his jaw tightening, then relaxing. Reaching over, he turned down the volume on the radio.

"It might be better if we keep it quiet for a while." Like he'd told her, she couldn't depend on him and he didn't want to put her in a difficult position with her family. "Kade already knows, and I'm pretty certain Matt has a suspicion. For now, I'd like to keep it that way."

"I think Cassie and Janie suspect something is going on. But you're right. This may burn out real quick. No sense making an issue of it." Her chest squeezed a little at the decision. She hated keeping secrets from her family.

After what he'd told her, she didn't blame Gage for being cautious. It just made it awkward around her family and friends to pretend they meant nothing to each other. The thought caused her heart to seize.

Skye already knew she'd developed strong feelings for him, more than she wanted or knew was safe. He'd made his priorities clear. He wasn't interested in a relationship with anyone, including her. Pretending they weren't together was easy for him because in his mind, they weren't. At least not in any traditional way. Somehow, hooking up didn't sound right, either.

She felt Gage's hand cover hers, his warmth taking the chill from her fingers.

"Look, Skye. If it's important to you, we can tell them." His words held no real conviction, confirming he truly did want to keep their time together a secret.

"No. I'm good with keeping it to ourselves. Besides, after this weekend, it could be weeks or months before we see each other again."

His hand tightened on hers. "Trust me, darlin'. It's not going to be weeks. I'll fly you down to Houston next weekend if you don't have plans."

Her heart skipped a few beats. Controlling her excitement, knowing anything could happen in a week, she looked over and smiled. "I'd love to fly down for a visit."

Following his GPS, he parked behind the trucks already in front of the Garner house. Leaning over, he cupped her face in both hands, kissing her until he was about ready to restart the engine and leave. Dropping his hands, he moved away, both of them taking ragged breaths.

"Guess we'd better get inside." Getting out, he let the cool night air chill his reaction to her. Opening her door, he held out his hand. At this rate, everyone would know they were together without either saying a word.

"Didn't you get in trouble?" Janie wiped the tears from her face. She hadn't stopped laughing since Nesto and Kade started telling stories of their time together in Special Forces.

"Don't believe a word either one says, Janie. They're famous for embellishing stories until the difference between truth and fantasy is miniscule." Brooke set down a tray of appetizers, dropping down next to Kade, sliding an arm around her husband's shoulders.

"The last story was almost completely true. Right, Kade?"

Stuffing a cracker with meat and cheese into his mouth, he nodded.

"And the others?" Janie asked.

"They were close, too." Nesto smiled over the rim of a glass of whiskey.

Matt stood a few feet away, holding a glass of scotch in his hand. "All right, you guys. Get yourselves in the dining room. The food's ready."

Nesto held out his hand, helping Janie up. "I haven't even *begun* to tell you stories about my days in the U.S. Marshal Service."

"They aren't nearly as interesting as the ones with me in them." Kade kept his arm around Brooke's waist, following Nesto and Janie to the table.

"You guys ought to write a book." Janie sat down, Nesto taking the seat next to her.

"Yeah. Maybe they'd make it into a movie." Matt pulled out Cassie's chair, then sat beside her.

"Where are Gage and Skye?" Kade glanced around, seeing no sign of them.

"Last I saw, they were out at the barn with Thunder." Matt picked up a bowl, passing it down the table.

"Who's Thunder?" Nesto placed a spoonful of potatoes on his plate.

"My horse. I've had him forever." Matt glanced at Cassie.

"He used to board him at the rodeo grounds in college. If Thunder was in his stall, I knew I'd find Matt around somewhere." What Cassie didn't say was finding Thunder gone their last year of college was the way she'd discovered Matt had graduated early, leaving for the rodeo without telling her. "I'll go get them."

"I'll go. I need to grab another drink anyway."

Kade walked through the kitchen and out the back door. They had a deep lot on the outskirts of Cold Creek, zoned for horses. He'd heard Matt and Cassie talking about getting her one. So far, only Thunder occupied the barn.

Hearing laughter, he walked through the barn door, stopping when he saw Gage and Skye, arms wrapped around each other. Clearing his throat louder than needed, he stepped closer as they jumped apart.

"Dinner's ready."

"Um…thanks, Kade." Skye walked past Gage, then Kade, on her way to the house.

When Gage followed, Kade walked alongside him.

"Don't say anything. This is between Skye and me." Seeing her step inside the house, he turned to Kade. "And don't say you'll kill me if I hurt her because I already know I'll be dealing with a slew of angry MacLarens if that happens…which is *not* my intention."

Kade clasped a hand on Gage's shoulder. "Easy, man. I'd never kill you. Slow torture would be my choice."

Gage snorted, holding the door open for Kade. "Thanks. That sounds so much better."

Gage stroked Skye's arm, her body draped over him, head resting on his chest. The ride back to the hotel after dinner had taken too long. All he could think about was getting her back to the room, doing everything he'd fantasized about all day, then keeping her in bed as long as she'd let him.

They had no agenda for Saturday or Sunday, hadn't even discussed if they'd spend the two days together. Both had planes to catch early Monday morning. If things crashed and burned, he knew the flights could be changed. He also knew that wouldn't happen.

His heart sped up at the feel of her hand skimming over his chest, playing with the silky hairs, her leg tightening possessively over his. Drawing in a breath, he let her explore, doing his best to stay calm and not take control. His natural instincts didn't make it easy.

Flinching as she placed kisses on his chest, then up his neck and along his jaw, he turned toward her, accepting her lips. They went slow, savoring each other, telling each what they wanted without speaking.

It had never been like this for him. Effortless, comfortable, as if he and Skye were meant to be together. He didn't linger on the notion as she straddled him, pushing all coherent thought from his mind.

"Sure. I can meet you there. What time?"

Gage sat across the room, listening as Skye spoke to Cassie on the phone. They'd already made plans to drive into the mountains, make a day of seeing the sights. She'd ordered lunch from a nearby deli. Sounded as if their day had changed.

"What's up?" he asked when she ended the call.

"Seems Heath's wife, Annie, wants to open a satellite office of the MacLaren Foundation in Crooked Tree."

His brows knit together. "The MacLaren Foundation?"

"It's a non-profit that raises money for foster kids leaving the system. They get a place to stay, help finding employment and applying for college. Some states stop foster payments when they reach eighteen, even if the kids still have several months left of high school to get their diploma. The foundation is a way to help them transition without relying on welfare. A chance they may not have otherwise. The headquarters is in Fire Mountain. Cassie opened a satellite office here in Cold Creek. Now Annie wants one in Crooked Tree."

"And who would run it?"

She choked out a laugh. "Me. Cassie handles the one here, so…"

"I'm guessing the kids get to work at one of the MacLaren companies."

"Part or full-time, depending on if they are also going to college. Most start at a community college, then transfer to a four-year. It saves costs and the kids get a chance to make sure it's what they want."

"Sounds like you aren't going to be able to see the sights with me."

"Don't even think about trying to get out of spending the day with me, Templeton. We're meeting Cassie at the local office in half an hour. Then we'll pick up our food and take off." She walked over to him, leaning forward, resting her hands on his shoulders. "Unless you've changed your mind."

Grabbing her around the waist, he tugged her onto his lap, giving her a slow kiss. "Not a chance, beautiful."

Laughing, she pushed away. "You don't mind doing this with me?"

"Not at all. Sounds like a great idea. The question is, are you okay with being seen with me?"

Grabbing a light jacket and her purse, she walked to the door. "She already suspects. If she asks, I don't want to lie." She hesitated, pushing away the knot in her throat. "When it ends, it ends. People see each other then call it off all the time. Don't worry. This won't commit you to anything."

Standing, Gage took three long strides, setting his hands on her shoulders. "I'm not worried about this ending, and you shouldn't be, either. As far as letting Cassie know we're seeing each other, it's fine with me. I'll just have to find a way to placate Matt when he doesn't hear it from me first." Placing a soft kiss on her parted lips, he opened the door. "Let's go meet Cassie, then get out of town. We could both use the break."

Cassie didn't ask questions as her gaze jumped between them when they walked into the MacLaren Foundation office.

"Thanks again for dinner last night, Cassie. It was great of you to include me." Gage stepped up to her, then leaned down to kiss her cheek.

"Of course. You're almost like, well…family." She grinned, then turned to pick up a folder on the desk. "This isn't much, but it will give you the basics of how I set up this place, as well as the pertinent data on the foundation. Annie will meet with you anytime, even fly up to Crooked Tree to help scout out an office."

Skye glanced at Cassie. "It can't be in an empty office at work?"

"The last time I was up there, I didn't see any empty offices."

"There is that. Kade and the brothers are working on plans to expand, but it won't happen for a year."

Skye glanced through the file, asked a few questions, then closed it. "I suppose I don't get a raise in salary if I take this on," she joked.

"That is the one piece of good news. There *is* a small salary included, separate from what you already make. Matt and I used mine to fix up the barn. So, what do you think?"

"It's a lot of work. I don't know how you do it, Cassie."

"I couldn't without Matt being so supportive. There are meetings at night and on weekends with volunteers and the kids who are about to lose support. Oh, and you get to work with Sean."

"My brother?"

"He's in charge of the summer program for foster kids at all our locations. It's for those between the ages of thirteen and seventeen. If they can come up with money for transportation, the camp is free. Food, lodging, activities. All they have to do is get close and Sean picks them up at the bus station, airport, train depot…wherever. Next summer, Matt's going to volunteer for a couple weeks. I think Mitch, Kade, Cam, Eric, and Rhett have offered to help, too." Cassie glanced at Gage, lowering her voice. "Maybe someday he'll get on the list."

Gage stood across the room, saying nothing, taking it all in. Even the whispered part about him someday helping at the summer camp. The thought intrigued him. He rolled it over in his mind, guessing he could still volunteer when what he had with Skye ended. Gage couldn't think of a reason she'd object.

Skye looked over at Gage, who seemed to be occupying himself by reading one of the brochures. "You know I'll be leaning on you a lot. It may require a few girls' nights. You know, to go over logistics, funding…" She smiled, liking the whole idea.

"Great. I'll call Annie and let her know you're in. She's going to be so happy. Oh, and Kade already knows about it."

Skye nodded. "Of course he does. If there's nothing else, Gage and I will take off."

Cassie lifted a brow. "Any special plans today?"

"Taking a drive in the mountains. You and Matt are welcome to come along."

"Thanks, but we have other plans." She absently placed a hand on her stomach.

Skye watched the action. It was the fourth time Cassie had done it over the last couple days. Add the fact her cousin hadn't had a drop of alcohol, and it brought up the obvious question.

"When's the baby due?"

Cassie's eyes grew wide, her mouth dropping open. "How did you know?"

"Cass, it wasn't too hard to figure out. Do Heath and Annie know?"

"No one knows, Skye. We want to wait for another doctor visit, then we'll fly to Fire Mountain to tell them."

Gage walked over, slinging an arm around Skye's shoulders. "You tell Matt congratulations for me."

Cassie winced, glancing at the ground, then back up at Gage. "He'd planned to tell you last night. There just didn't seem to be a good time."

"No problem. Family should come first. Have him call me when he gets back to Cold Creek." He looked at Skye. "Are you ready?"

"I am."

"Then let's get up in those mountains."

Chapter Fourteen

Fire Mountain

Kade, Brooke, and Nesto stood at the edge of the tarmac, waiting for the plane carrying Reyna and Ivan. Rafe sat in the large SUV in the parking lot, his hands gripping the steering wheel as he stared up at the sky.

"Why doesn't he wait here with us?" Brooke took a quick glance over her shoulder. "It's obvious he's worried about her."

Kade shoved his hands into his pockets, blowing out a breath as he shook his head. "I've never been able to figure out what goes on in my father's head."

Brooke laid a hand on his shoulder. "Have you talked to him about your mother? Maybe he'd open up if you did."

Snorting, he looked over his shoulder at the SUV. "Get in touch with our feelings, Brooke? I don't think so. We're doing our best to heal what happened in the past. Like anything else, it's a slow process."

"There it is, Kade." Nesto focused his attention on a plane coming from the east. "Looks like a Gulfstream G450. The Santiago family must be doing well."

Kade shifted his gaze from the plane to Nesto. "I never knew you were an expert on private jets."

"I rode in a few with the marshal service. It isn't normal protocol, but hey, I didn't complain."

"What does something like that cost?"

Nesto smiled. "It's the same plane your family owns, Brooke. Bought new, they're somewhere around forty million. The next step up costs close to twenty million more."

"Really? I had no idea the jet cost that much."

"Plus, there's the helicopter, Brooke. Two different pilots, although Cam is certified for both. He's been pushing me to learn." Kade shook his head at the notion.

"If the company needs another pilot and pays for the training, why not?" Brooke looked at her husband. Kade was an adrenaline junky. Anything fast, most likely dangerous, always caught his attention.

"Weekend training, so we'd hardly see each other at all. I've got my bike. She's all I need when I've got the urge for speed." Kade looked over Brooke's shoulder at Nesto, seeing his friend nod.

"It's landing." Brooke slid her hand into Kade's, feeling him tighten his grip. She leaned toward him. "Your mother coming here may turn out to be good in many ways."

Keeping his focus on the plane, Kade shrugged. "Right now, all I care about is my mother being safe. Anything beyond that is between her and Rafe."

She could see his Adam's apple bob a little, wondering if getting his parents together meant more to Kade than he cared to admit.

Ivan came down the steps first, followed by Reyna and two other men.

"Bodyguards?" Kade asked.

Nesto narrowed his gaze on the men. "Looks like it. I'd do the same if it were me."

Brooke let go of his hand. "Guess you'd better get out there."

Not replying, he jogged out to meet Reyna, wrapping his mother in his arms. "I'm glad you're here."

She returned the hug, then stepped back. "It was an adventure I'd prefer not to repeat." Looking around him, she smiled at the two familiar faces walking up. "Ah, Nesto. It's good to see you."

He stepped into her open arms. "It's good to see you, too. We've all been worried about you, Mama Reyna." He used the endearment she'd insisted on when he and Kade became friends. Nesto moved aside to let Brooke give her mother-in-law a hug.

"It's wonderful to have you here. I just wish it were under different circumstances."

Brooke turned at the sound of a car door closing. Rafe pushed his cowboy hat lower on his head, making his way to the plane. Without acknowledging Reyna, he walked up to where Ivan, Kade, and Nesto talked.

Rafe extended his hand. "Ivan. Thank you for bringing Kade's mother here."

"It's the best place for her. I know your family will let nothing happen."

Rafe looked over his shoulder, seeing the women walk toward them. "I give you my word. Nothing will happen to Reyna."

"I will hold you to that." Ivan's words were accompanied by an intense, level gaze.

Turning, Rafe sucked in a slow breath as Reyna stopped a couple feet away.

"Hello, Rafe. Thank you for agreeing to let me stay here with your family."

"You're always welcome here, Reyna. You've never needed an excuse." He let his gaze wander over her. "You look well."

Her eyes crinkled at the corners. "Is that a polite way of saying I'm older, but maturing nicely?"

He cocked his head to the side. "Are you fishing for compliments?"

"Never. One look in a mirror and a woman knows what has changed. I'm not the same as I was all those years ago. You, though, look the same. Still tall and trim."

"You forgot handsome."

"Ah, Rafe. You will never change, and neither will your son. Cocky and arrogant."

He looked at her, his face sobering. "*Our* son, Reyna. Kade belongs to both of us."

Her lips parted, as if she wanted to respond, then tightened into a thin line when Ivan stepped next to her.

"Where should we put Aunt Reyna's luggage?" he asked.

Rafe looked at the baggage carrier, raising a brow. "Only three bags?"

She shrugged. "I brought what I would need for a few weeks."

Nodding, he indicated the SUV. "They'll fit easily into the back." Offering his arm to Reyna, he let out a breath when she slid her hand through it. "It won't take long to get to the ranch. Annie has lunch prepared for everyone."

Kade watched them walk off, feeling Brooke thread her fingers through his. He looked at Nesto standing on his other side, his friend's face a mask.

"Looks like they're ready to leave." Kade started off, the two people he trusted completely with him. He felt somewhat like a child watching his mother and father, as if seeing them together were an everyday occurrence.

For an instant, he wondered what it would've been like to grow up in a home with the three of them together. Kade ruthlessly pushed the thought aside. He was no longer a child lying awake at night, wondering what had happened to his father, why the man didn't want him or his mother. Real life was so much more complicated than a child could grasp. He wondered if it had seemed the same all those years ago when Rafe and Reyna went their separate ways.

Cold Creek

"These early morning flights are hell," Gage mumbled as he took the towel from Skye's hand, drying her shoulders and back.

"We could've both flown out last night." She turned in his arms. "Saved you from getting up at such a ridiculous hour."

He tightened his hold, kissing her forehead, capturing her lips. On Saturday morning, they seemed to have all the time in the world. Two full days and nights. Monday had seemed too far off to think about.

"You're going to make us miss our flights," Skye whispered against his mouth, then stepped away. Taking the towel from him, she hung it over the bar, picking up her brush. She heard the phone the same time he did.

"It's mine." Gage grabbed it. "Hello, Ivan. Did you get Reyna to Fire Mountain?" It wasn't unusual for him to call well before most people were awake.

"We're both here. We arrived an hour ago."

"How is she doing?" Gage glanced behind him, then turned, watching Skye dry her hair. Something had shifted this weekend. It had happened a little more each hour they'd spent together. She'd chipped away at the wall he'd built, the barriers to his heart he thought were too strong to crack.

"Reyna is doing well. Rafe was at the airport with Kade, Brooke, and Nesto. He assured me she could stay as long as she wanted."

"They'll keep her safe, Ivan. It's doubtful anyone outside your family knows about the MacLarens or her connection to them." Gage couldn't seem to drag his eyes away from Skye. The peace he felt being around her had been unexpected, a gift he'd never had before, didn't know he'd been missing.

"I'll be leaving for El Paso in the morning. Unless something unexpected comes up, I have no plans to fly to Houston before returning to León."

"Gonzo and Daria know to call me if anything happens. I've heard from neither." He checked the time. They had to leave in ten minutes and he hadn't dressed or packed. "I've a flight to catch, Ivan. I'll let you know if anything changes in Houston." He set the phone on the bed.

"You're not ready." Skye didn't hide her interest in his current state of undress, a smile spreading across her face.

"Give me five minutes."

Grabbing his pants off a chair, he made quick work of slipping into his clothes and stuffing the remainder of his belongings into his bag. He'd checked out of his room Saturday morning, knowing if things didn't go well with Skye, he'd fly back to Houston early. "Ready?"

Skye looked around, taking her time to make sure they'd left nothing behind. Sighing, she looked at him. "Yes. I'm ready."

They took the elevator down, then waited outside for the shuttle, neither saying a word. When the van pulled up, Gage took Skye's bag from her hand, motioning her to get in, taking a seat next to her. Between the time they'd gotten out of the shower and now, a chill had formed around them. Gage didn't question why. Instead, he reached over and grabbed her hand, placing it in his lap.

Both remained silent as they checked in at the counter, passed through security, and made their way to the gates. Their flights were on the same airline, thirty minutes apart. Skye would leave first. They'd already talked about her flying to Houston the following weekend, only four days away.

"I could use some coffee. How about you?" Gage set his bag down.

"A latte would be great. Thanks." Taking a seat, Skye watched him walk away, already feeling a sense of loss. Given the fact they'd be seeing each other again in a few days, her reaction made no sense. All morning, she'd expected him to tell her he'd changed his mind, saying it had been fun, but it was over. There were times she could read him, guess his thoughts. Most of the time, though, he held himself apart, making it impossible to get a real sense of his true feelings.

Fun and casual, she reminded herself as he approached, a coffee in each hand. Skye had to admit they had fun, laughing and sharing stories of their childhoods. Their time in bed, at the picnic, in the shower had been more than her most vivid fantasies. If she were being honest, he'd ruined her for anyone else.

Looking at him, her heart thudded. If, like some of her friends, she kept a list of characteristics required to commit to a man, Gage would possess each one. She'd fallen in love with him over a few weeks and one incredible weekend. It was too much, too soon, and not at all what they agreed to.

"Here you go." He handed her the cup, wariness replacing his normal smile. Sitting down, he again took her hand. "Are you still up for seeing me this weekend?"

A little of the tension seeped out of her. She took a sip of her latte and smiled. "I am. Do you want me to make the arrangements?"

"I'll do it. How about flying in late Friday afternoon, leaving early Monday?"

Groaning, she gave him a playful punch in the arm. "You like to see me at my worst, don't you?"

"Hey. I have to get up at the same time to drive you to the airport." Drinking his coffee, Gage broached a subject he hadn't tackled in a long time. "Do you have any objections to staying at my place?"

His question surprised her. She'd expected Gage to set her up in a hotel, keeping her away from his personal space.

"Well, I don't know. Do you have to move out some other woman's clothes before I get there?" She could tell by the look on his face Gage knew she only half teased him.

"I've never invited a woman to my house, Skye."

Straightening in her seat, she leaned toward him. "Why me, Gage?"

He shook his head. "Damned if I know." He tried to smile, failing miserably.

"You don't have to do this. I can get a hotel room and you can stay with me. If things go sour, then…" Her voice stalled as her throat constricted.

Gage grabbed her chin, lifting it so she had to look at him. "Don't go borrowing trouble. I invited you to stay at my place and I meant it. There'll be no hotel this weekend." Leaning down, he kissed her before releasing his grip.

The announcement of her flight had them standing, her juggling a carry-on, purse, and coffee.

"I had a great time this weekend."

Smiling at her, he brushed another kiss across her lips. "Then I guess we'll have to work extra hard to make next weekend even better."

Getting in line, Skye took one more look at him before entering the gangway. Finding her seat, she stowed her bag in the overhead and her purse under the seat in front of her. Securing the seat belt, she leaned back, holding her cup in both hands.

She wanted to believe Gage felt the same connection she did and looked forward to seeing her again in a few days. His words and actions confirmed he did. Without conscious thought, doubt formed, finding a place to settle deep inside her. It wouldn't be safe to read too much into the behavior of a man clearly in lust. Once the newness wore off, she had to remember he'd be gone.

Drinking more of her latte, she winced. The pleasant sweetness had turned bitter, the agreeable aftertaste sour. Closing her eyes, Skye did the one thing she could control— letting her mind drift back over the weekend. As the plane took off, she fell asleep to a memory of being wrapped in his arms, his warm lips trailing a heated path over her body.

Gage settled in his seat, waiting to secure his seat belt, when a young woman stopped next to him, motioning toward the window seat. Standing, he let her slide in, noticing the way her jeans and blouse molded to her body, her deep auburn hair falling around her shoulders, the smile she shot him.

Instead of being tempted to engage in conversation, his mind shifted to Skye, a slight grin playing across his face. The weekend couldn't have gone better, although their parting hadn't been as smooth as he'd hoped. Then he'd asked her to stay at his house, a gesture that still surprised him.

Gage never invited women to his home, preferring to go to their place or get a room in a nearby hotel. Something was seriously messed up with him and he didn't know what to do about it, other than cool things off. The thought gave him none of the comfort he expected. He wanted Skye in his house, in his bed, sharing a part of him he'd offered no other woman since his divorce.

"Excuse me. I wonder if I could read the magazine. There doesn't seem to be one at my seat." The woman next to him gestured to the pocket of the seat in front of him.

"Sure." Pulling it out, he handed it to her. That's when he noticed the strong resemblance to Cassie.

"My name's Nicole." She held out her hand.

"Gage." Gripping her hand, he smiled.

"Do you live in Houston?"

"I do. You?"

"Near Austin. I'm taking a break from college in Colorado, visiting a friend in Houston for a few days before going home. I figure I'll get a job, then decide what's next."

Gage figured her to be twenty, maybe twenty-one. At thirty-four, it made him feel old. "The job market is pretty good right now. I doubt you'll have a problem."

She shrugged. "I should be fine. I've got my bachelor's, but ran out of steam on my MBA. My head wasn't in it."

Which meant she was probably closer to twenty-two or twenty-three. It still made him feel old. "What's your degree in?"

"Accounting. My folks own a ranch. My brothers have their degrees and work for the family. I hope to do the same."

"Keeping the family business going. I can understand that." He reached into his pocket, pulling out a card. "Tell you what. Send me your résumé. I don't know if I can help, but I do know a few people around Houston."

Her face brightened as she took his card. Searching her purse, she found one of her own. "It's not much, but it's got my address and email."

Gage took it, sliding the card into his shirt pocket without reading the information. "You'll probably find something right off."

"I've got a big family. They're all involved in ranching one way or another. I'm not too worried." She turned, looking out the window.

Gage leaned back in his seat, closing his eyes. He'd called Gonzo before boarding, letting him know Ivan's itinerary. Nothing had happened while Gage had been out of town. Daria had called in sick, which was unusual. She hadn't missed a day since she'd started. If that were the worst of it, Gage figured he'd have a pretty easy week.

When he got back, he'd call Thad, find out if he'd learned any more from his contacts. He hoped his friend had heard nothing, which could mean he and Ivan were worried about nothing. The only real red flag had been the feds showing up. They'd never really had any concrete evidence the trucking company was involved in anything illegal. With Reyna and Ivan's mother in safe locations, Ivan would have one less thing to worry about, which meant a lot to Gage. They had a big year coming up. Everyone needed to focus on the business, not on suspicions they couldn't confirm.

Sliding his hat low on his forehead, his thoughts turned to Skye. He'd see her in four days, already wishing it were sooner. He let out a breath. Yep, something was really messed up.

Chapter Fifteen

Fire Mountain

"I can't tell you how much I appreciate your help, Reyna." Annie MacLaren rolled out the crust for another pie. "With Kade, Brooke, Matt, and Cassie staying an extra day, it's like feeding an army."

"Cooking is my therapy, Annie. It is always good to prepare food for people who enjoy it." Reyna followed the recipe for the fresh fruit filling, making enough for two pies.

"I know what you mean. Heath used to have a cook. When she retired, I volunteered to take over." She wiped her hands on her apron, then laughed. "I had no idea what I was getting myself into. Heath loves to entertain. It's a rare week when we don't have people over at least two nights. Tonight, we have a good number of the family here."

"You may have to help me with names." Reyna wiped her sleeve across her brow. "I worry I will embarrass Rafe or one of his children."

Annie stopped and turned toward her. "Please, don't ever worry about embarrassing any of us. We're a large clan. Sometimes, it's even hard for me." Walking over to her, Annie leaned against the counter. "How are you doing, Reyna? This must be difficult for you."

Stirring the fruit filling, Reyna considered her answer. "You and your family have been very kind, allowing me to stay here."

Annie nodded. "We're pleased to have you. We think the world of Kade. You did a wonderful job raising him by yourself. I'm not sure I could've done it."

"I don't know you well, but I am certain you would've been fine. Like me, you would not have had a choice." Reyna set the pan on the stove, turned on the flame, and continued to stir. "Even though my father forbid the family to contact me, my brother, Javier, sent money as often as he could. You have to remember, he was a young man at the time, without the wealth he has today. What he sent meant I could pay rent each month. I don't know if my other brothers or our father ever learned of what he did."

"Did you ever think of asking Rafe for help?"

The spoon in Reyna's hand stilled. Sucking in a slow breath, she looked at Annie. "Yes, more than you'd think. I could never go through with it. When Kade was a boy, Rafe saw us in a restaurant. It was the first time we'd seen each other in years. I saw the look on his face when he spotted Kade. He knew, Annie." Her voice cracked. Clearing her throat, she focused on her task. "He knew Kade was his and did not come near us, never tried to find me. After that, how could I approach him? His actions made it clear he wanted nothing to do with us."

Annie touched Reyna's arm. "Perhaps he didn't know. Maybe he thought you were married and had a son."

"You are a kind soul, Annie." She shook her head, a wave of sorrow washing over her. "Kade looked exactly like Rafe did as a boy. When we were together, he'd given me a few photos of him. One was when he was about Kade's age when he saw us in the restaurant. The horror on his face when he saw Kade broke my heart. I knew then he'd never acknowledge his son."

"People change, Reyna. Rafe wants nothing more than to build a relationship with his son."

"And I am glad for that. I hope Kade will find it in his heart one day to forgive his father."

"Do you think you could ever do the same, Reyna?"

Turning off the heat to the bubbling mixture, she took the pan off the stove, setting it on a trivet. Ignoring the ball of tension building in her chest, she looked at Annie, ready to reply when Rafe walked in.

"Smells good." His deep, rough voice had them both staring. He looked around the kitchen, then settled his narrowed gaze on Reyna. "She has you working?"

Reyna lifted her chin, her face devoid of expression. "I volunteered. Besides, I'm not happy sitting around, doing nothing."

Rafe snorted. "Right. I'm sure Javier has you cooking and cleaning." Sarcasm dripped from his voice. Leaning against the counter, he crossed his arms. "Let me guess. You have five, six servants in León? What do you do each day? Shop? Perhaps spend time with a—"

Annie stiffened. "Rafe. That's enough."

Pushing away from the counter, he dropped his arms, running a hand through his hair. "You're right. I apologize, Reyna. I was out of line."

Reyna shrugged, turning away, but not before Annie saw tears pooling in her eyes.

"How's it going in here?" Kade walked in, coming to an abrupt halt when he took in the scene. He knew enough to sense something had happened. Turning to Rafe, he took a step forward, his voice harsh. "What did you say to her?"

Rafe blew out a breath. "I—"

"It is fine, Kade. Your father was just asking me about dinner."

He walked over to his mother, setting a hand on her shoulder. "Is that why you have tears in your eyes?"

Rafe moved closer, his voice low, controlled. "I am sorry, Reyna."

She shook her head, looking at Kade, then Rafe. "It is all right. There has been much going on, and it is always hard to be away from home. Perhaps I should go lie down for a while."

"I'll walk you up to your room, Mother."

She looked at Annie. "Do you mind? I'll come down to help finish."

"I don't mind at all. Take as much time as you need. I'll send Kade or Brooke up when we're ready to eat."

"Come on, Mother." Kade shot an angry glare at Rafe, then turned his back on him, escorting his mother to the stairs.

Annie spun toward Rafe. "Reyna was kidnapped, sent here for safety, and *you* were the one who spoke to Heath on her behalf." Annie's anger would've been hard to miss. "What in the world were you thinking?"

Rubbing a hand down his face, he paced a few feet away, then turned. "Hell, I don't know. It all just came out."

Picking up a wooden spoon, she shook it at him. "If it happens again, grown man or not, I promise I'll use this on you." Returning to her pies, she set the spoon down, hearing Rafe's heavy footsteps as he left the room.

Kade stalked outside toward Rafe, not stopping until he stood a foot away. He glanced around, glad to see no one else. "I want to know what you said to her. She's a strong woman who never cries. She won't tell me anything, so I've come to hear it from you."

A muscle ticked in Rafe's jaw, his mouth tight and grim. "What goes on between your mother and me is none of your business." As he started to turn away, Kade's hand clamped down on his arm. If it had been anyone else, Rafe would have been tempted to land a blow to the man's jaw.

Kade's nostrils flared, his eyes burning with anger. "Everything that goes on with *my* mother *is* my business, especially when it involves the man who walked away from her. From us." He dropped his hold, turning to pace away. "I should take her away. Having her stay here was a bad idea." He could hear Rafe move up behind him, but didn't turn around.

"I made a comment about her life in León with servants, cooks, and drivers. It was thoughtless and unkind. She wanted to help Annie with dinner, and I…" Rafe wished he could change what had been said. He hated himself for allowing the pain they'd caused each other years before to surface.

Placing fisted hands on his hips, Kade looked at the ground, shaking his head. "When I was growing up, she worked no less than two jobs to keep food on the table and give us a place to live. We didn't have much, but she made sure it was clean, that my clothes and shoes didn't have holes. Not once did she complain…or cry." Lifting his head, he turned slowly, his eyes flashing with pain and anger. "My grandfather wouldn't allow anyone to help her. He never invited her home, and had no interest in meeting me. The only one who helped was Uncle Javier, Ivan's father. When I was eight, I started working, doing whatever anyone would pay me to do. Nights, weekends, and school breaks were all spent working. I didn't mind, though. All I wanted was to help my mother."

Rafe's throat pulsed with emotion. "I didn't know."

"Maybe not at first, but I *know* you figured it out when you saw Mother and me in the restaurant." Kade walked to a nearby bench and sat down. "It wasn't until my thirteenth birthday that I learned you were my father. Mother asked me to get something under her bed, forgetting what she'd hidden in an old shoebox. My birth certificate was inside. You were listed as my father. She had told me my father's last name was Taylor and had died." He let out a defeated breath. "When I confronted her, she told me about you seeing us a few years before. The fact you didn't come forward, didn't want anything to do with me, told me everything I needed to know about you."

Rafe lowered himself on the other end of the bench, leaning forward, his arms resting on his legs. "Reyna and I had a complicated situation. Her father hated me, so we avoided her family, seeing each other whenever and wherever we could. One night, she didn't show up. When it happened again the next night, I went looking for her." He stared at the ground, shaking his head slowly. "They were gone. The house was empty. I hoped she'd contact me, but I never heard from her. The first time I saw her again was in the restaurant." Straightening, he looked at Kade. "You must have been five, maybe six. You're right. In that instant, I knew you were mine, yet I did nothing." Standing, Rafe took a few steps away, then turned. "I had asked Deidra to marry me. She was with me that night." He moved closer to Kade. "I'll never be able to make up for not walking over to you, confirming you were mine. All I can do is try to make up for it."

"She never told you about being pregnant?"

He shook his head, a bitter laugh escaping. "I asked her to marry me…more than once. She refused, knowing her father would never agree. I'm guessing when Reyna found out she was pregnant, her family moved, got her as far away from me as they could. Until that day in the restaurant, it never occurred to me they'd moved just a few miles away."

Pushing himself up, Kade glanced around, then looked at Rafe. "What's done is done." Starting to walk away, he stopped at Rafe's words.

"You're my son, Kade. There isn't a straw's width of difference between the love I have for you and my other children."

"And Mother? How do you feel about her?"

Rafe sucked in an unsteady breath. So much had happened between them. Her betrayal at not finding him, telling him about Kade. His inaction, refusing to acknowledge their son when he had the chance. The pain they'd inflicted on each other ran deep, even after more than thirty years. Shaking his head, his weary gaze met Kade's.

"It's all right. You and Mother will figure it out."

Houston

"I'll be out the rest of the day, Daria."

"Wait, Gage. You have a message." Daria held it out to him. "It's from your brother, Brent. I think he also called last week when you were in Cold Creek, but didn't leave a message. Said he'd call back."

Gage took the paper, folding and slipping it into a pocket without reading the message.

Daria watched his actions and leaned forward. "He said it was important."

He waved a hand in the air as he walked to the door. "I'll call him. Right now, I have a plane to meet at the airport."

Stepping outside, he shrugged out of his lightweight jacket, slinging it over his shoulder. The air felt warm with little humidity—at least by Houston standards. The weekend forecast was for the same, which worked well with his plans. Starting the truck, he pulled onto the street, glancing up. It was a perfect day for Skye to fly into the city.

He'd spent last night cleaning up, changing the sheets, and stocking his refrigerator with something other than leftover takeout and beer. Tonight, he'd cook at home. Tomorrow, they'd go to a friend's ranch not far from town. The man and his family lived in San Antonio, coming to Houston every few months. A ranch manager and a couple men took care of the place, but his friend had offered Gage a standing invitation to come out and ride whenever he wanted. Afterward, they'd drive south to Galveston. Skye had mentioned wanting to see the town, so he'd rented a beachfront cottage for the night. Maybe they'd come for longer someday.

Scanning the curb at the arrival terminal, he couldn't miss her waiting with a bag, her long blonde hair pulled into a ponytail. Flashing his lights, Gage pulled over and jumped out. Taking her bag, he placed it in the back seat, then put an arm around Skye's waist, pulling her to him.

"I'm glad you came." The kiss he'd intended to be short, a brush of the lips, heated quickly, Skye wrapping her arms around his neck.

"Thanks for the invitation," she whispered against his lips.

"I guess we should get going." He could have stood there all afternoon, ignoring the curious glances of the people walking past.

"I guess so..."

Taking a reluctant step back, he opened the door, letting her slide in before leaning down for one more kiss. "We'll head to my place, let you get settled."

Closing the door, he walked around to his side, hoping it didn't take her long to unwind from the flight. He'd planned a lot of time with her in his bed before tackling dinner.

"Let's take a shower, then I'll make us something to eat." Gage reached down, grinning as he helped untangle the sheets wrapped around her legs. "You got pretty wild."

Sitting up, she looked at his naked body, a fresh wave of desire spreading through her. "I had good reason to be." Before she could say more, Gage bent down, lifting her.

"That so?"

Burying her face in his neck, she sighed. "Are you sure you're hungry?"

"Are you kidding? With the way you attacked me, I'll need as much nourishment as I can get this weekend."

Lowering his head, he claimed her lips, crushing her to him. Her warm, moist mouth ignited a renewed wave of desire. Growling, his tongue traced the soft fullness of her lips before he deepened the kiss. After being in bed for several hours, making love over and over, he couldn't believe his body was ready to go again.

Lifting his head, he set her down, stroking a hand down her face. "I'll start the shower."

Skye watched him walk away, admiring his toned muscles. Shaking her head, she grabbed a few items from her bag, glancing at the dresser as she walked past. Her eyes caught on a business card placed to one side, the name jumping out at her. Picking it up, her stomach tightened.

"You coming?" Gage poked his head out of the bath, seeing her hold the card up.

"Where did you get this?"

Walking over, he took it from her hand without looking at it. "I sat next to Nicole on the trip back to Houston. She's taking a break from college, looking for a job. I told her to send me a résumé. Why?"

She cocked her head. "Did you even read it?"

"Well, not really." He held it up, focusing on it for the first time. "Nicole…" Gage looked at Skye, then back at the card. "MacLaren."

"My cousin, Nikki."

"Your cousin? Average height, slim, hair the color of…" He closed his eyes for an instant. "Hair the color of Cassie's. That's what I thought when I saw her. I had no idea there were more MacLarens."

She plucked the card from his hand, reading it again. "That's because we don't see them much. The fact is, my dad split off from the family before we were born. He didn't have much contact with those in Arizona. There are a few in California and some in Texas. It's a long story. I'll tell you what I know while we fix dinner."

He watched as she set the card back down on the dresser, wondering what other mysteries were hidden in the maze of MacLarens.

Chapter Sixteen

"I'd have to talk to Heath and Jace to get the whole story. What I remember is, way back, a group of MacLarens settled in Fire Mountain. Another part of the family settled in California, near Boundary Mountain. In the late eighteen hundreds, a small group from California left for Texas, buying land around Austin." Skye sliced a tomato, popping an olive into her mouth. "Those of us raised in Montana are just now learning about the others. I met Nikki, her parents, and brothers because they came to Cassie's wedding. I know there is at least one other family in Austin, but there could be more." She shrugged, dumping the tomatoes into the salad bowl. "I know very little about the ones in California."

Gage took the pan of chicken enchiladas out of the oven, placing it on the stovetop and tossing the pot holders aside. Crossing his arms, he leaned against the counter. "You have a huge family."

"Annie and Heath talked about a family reunion. I can't imagine the logistics of getting everyone together. They want to do it at the ranch in Fire Mountain." Picking up her glass of wine, she took a sip. "I know it would be a lot of work, but I think a reunion would be worth it. It's important to keep in touch with family."

Her words settled in Gage's chest, squeezing. The message from Brent still sat in a pocket of the shirt he'd worn today. It was the second time his brother had tried to reach him. Four years had passed since he'd walked in on him and Gwen, yet he still couldn't find it in himself to forgive Brent. If what he called about truly was important, Gage knew he'd have to talk to him, at least find out what he wanted.

"You all right?" Skye nudged his shoulder, rocking him out of his thoughts.

"Fine. Thinking about what it would look like with a field of MacLarens spread across the front yard of the ranch." Taking the pan of enchiladas from the stove, he grabbed the wine and headed for the dining room, Skye behind him with the salad. "Maybe you should call Annie. Tell her you'd like to help."

Skye almost choked on her wine. "Oh no. I'll leave that to her and Jace's wife. I've already committed to opening an office of the Maclaren Foundation in Crooked Tree. Until that's done and operating, I'm not taking any more on."

Dinner passed quietly, neither one talking much as they ate. Picking up the bottle of wine, Skye nodded toward his glass, filling it when he held it out to her.

"Do we have plans tomorrow?"

Leaning back in his chair, Gage rolled the stem of the glass between his fingers. "We do. How long since you've been on a trail ride?"

Her eyes widened. "Geez, really? I haven't been able to ride in weeks. I didn't know you had horses."

Gage explained what he planned, finishing with them staying in Galveston for the night. "What do you think?"

"Are you kidding? It sounds perfect." Setting her glass down, Skye stood, leaning down to kiss him.

"Like it that much, do you?" Grabbing her around the waist, he pulled her onto his lap. "How much do you like it?" His hands began to wander over her, unsnapping the front of the shirt she'd asked to wear.

"A lot," she groaned as his hands slid over her skin.

"A whole lot?"

"Oh yeah," she breathed against his mouth. "A whole lot."

The trails around the ranch were lush and isolated. Along with the beautiful weather, in Skye's opinion, that made the ride perfect.

"We'll stop up here to eat." Gage rode next to her, admiring the way she looked on the large gelding.

"What did you do with your horse?"

"My horse?" Gage's brows furrowed.

Skye looked at him. "The one you had when you competed."

"I left him at my folk's ranch when I started competing. Figured since I was riding bareback and saddle bronc, I didn't need to trailer a horse around. The last time I was there, he was doing fine."

"How long since you've been home?"

He thought a moment, feeling a thread of guilt. "Too long. A little over two years. I need to go home soon, see how they're doing."

"Where is home, Gage?" She knew of his divorce and the situation with his brother, but he'd never spoken of where he'd grown up.

"Oklahoma. My parents have a small spread with a few cattle and horses. Dad worked as an electrician to make ends meet. Mom worked in the high school library." He knew the ranch would go to him and Brent someday. "In case you're wondering, I don't have any cousins. It was always just the four of us."

Another mile went by before Gage pulled his horse to a stop at the top of a tree-covered trail. "This is it." Getting down, he opened the saddlebags, grabbing the food. "Bring the blanket." He nodded to the one tied behind her saddle.

"I have the drinks." She walked alongside him to a clearing a few yards from the trail. "It's so beautiful here. Do you get a chance to ride much?"

"Not as much as I'd like. Work is pretty demanding, and we're still a man short."

"I thought Matt said you had a replacement." She didn't like the idea of someone else taking over the clients Gage handled since Matt accepted the job with her family.

"He had some personal issues that have stretched on for months. A week ago, he called, saying he'd have to back off. So I'm starting again. I've got a few interviews this coming week."

Skye nodded. "I guess that means you won't be working with us anymore." She didn't look at him, didn't want to see the relief on his face at not having to travel so much.

Gage watched her, sensing more to her comment than having to do with a new employee. "I've been thinking. I might keep the MacLaren account for myself."

Her gaze snapped up to his, her mouth quirking up at the corners. "That would be great."

Setting down his plate, he leaned forward, pressing a kiss to her lips. "You aren't going to get rid of me that easily." He suppressed a wince the instant the words left his mouth. Somehow, they felt right, yet he still couldn't see himself committing a second time. He also couldn't picture a future without Skye. Gage felt as if he'd been caught in a web from which there was no easy escape.

Skye watched a series of emotions play over Gage's face. Desire, concern, perhaps fear all melded together before he masked it with a slow grin. He was as complicated a man as she'd ever met, with many layers and deep emotions.

"I'm not looking to get rid of you." She scooted closer, laying a hand on top of his. "Just trying to figure you out."

A deep, rich laugh exploded from his chest. "Honey, I'm a simple man. I enjoy work, good whiskey, rare steak, and an interesting woman. Right now, I couldn't ask for more." Standing, he held out his hand. "We'd better get going while we still have plenty of light. We've still got an hour drive to Galveston."

Packing everything away, they swung into their saddles and headed back. Gage turned her admission over in his mind. Gwen had never tried to understand him. Skye admitting it was something new.

He'd hidden nothing from her. Not his ugly divorce or the reason for it. What she didn't know concerned his work, and for good reason. Word getting out about them being watched by the government could set them back months, perhaps years. The fact they hadn't done anything wrong didn't matter. Most people were eager to embrace the worst. Their competitors would certainly use it to their advantage.

Double Ace didn't need what appeared to be their most lucrative partnership to learn of the raid. The MacLarens could be the ticket they needed to rise to the top of the bucking stock industry.

He thought back to a few months before when Thad had done three separate searches of trucks using a detection dog. He'd found nothing, the same as the searches Gage's employees had performed in the last weeks. The same as the feds found when they paid their visit. Still, Gage's instincts told him something was going on, and a part of him suspected Ivan's uncles were involved.

Gage wished he could talk openly with Kade. As a former DEA agent, the same as Thad, he might have additional ideas. Or he might tell him he'd watched too many television dramas about drug trafficking from Mexico. Gage snickered. Maybe he had. Before Skye, he'd spent more nights than he could count eating cheap takeout in front of the television, watching police dramas and stories about the U.S. Border Patrol.

Before Skye, he thought. Gage couldn't remember the last time he'd thought about having a particular woman in his life. He had to figure this all out before either one got in too deep, which meant he had to have some serious discussions with himself soon.

Fire Mountain

"Hey, Thad. I was hoping to catch you." Kade sat at a desk in MacLaren Enterprises headquarters. He'd decided to stay at least another week in Fire Mountain with Brooke and his mother before returning to Crooked Tree.

"Sounds like the voice of a ghost I haven't heard from in much too long. How are you, Taylor?"

"Doing pretty good. I don't know if you heard, but I got married."

"I did hear something about you giving it up for one woman. Such a shame. We used to have some good times before you went deep cover with that motorcycle gang."

Kade grimaced, remembering his life undercover as a member of the murderous gang, Satan's Brethren. He'd seen things, done things he regretted, but it had ended in the leaders going to prison.

"That's when it ended for me, Thad."

"Yeah. I knew you retired to work on a ranch in Arizona. From motorcycles to horses. Must've been a helluva transition." Thad's throaty laugh came through the phone.

"There's a lot more to it than that. It's why I called you."

Thad's jovial mood sobered. "Talk to me, man."

"Hold on a minute." Kade walked to the office door and closed it. "I work for the MacLarens now. Ever hear of them?"

"Hell yeah, I've heard of them. A ranching family with their hands in everything…cattle, horses, bucking stock, real estate. How'd you get hooked up with them?"

There was no humor in Kade's chuckle. "Turns out my father is a MacLaren."

"No shit."

"As God is my witness, brother. Most times, I've even started getting used to going by Kade MacLaren."

"Strange things and all that. What's that got to do with me?"

"Ivan Santiago. Do you know him?"

"I know *of* him. His family is involved in a bunch of stuff in Mexico. Some legitimate, some not. You must already know they're the major owners of Double Ace in Houston."

"Let me read you into the situation so we're on the same page. Reyna Santiago is my mother. Ivan is my cousin. And, as of a couple weeks ago, Gage Templeton is in thick with my sister, Skye. I understand you might know him. Is this getting to be too much for you?"

"Hold on a minute while I make a family tree," Thad shot back.

"I need to know what's going on with Double Ace."

Thad stayed silent as he thought over Kade's request. He wanted to share what he'd learned, but he owed Gage a certain amount of loyalty.

"You're putting me in an awkward position."

"Why's that?" Kade took the phone off speaker, picking up the handset.

"Gage and I are friends. I've been helping with some, uh…issues at work."

Kade understood loyalty. "What can you tell me?"

"First, how did you get dialed in on this, Kade?"

"My mother and Ivan's mother were kidnapped a couple weeks ago in León. They were released the next day. We figure it was done by either the de la Garza cartel or the Montalvo-Ortiz cartel."

"Shit," Thad muttered. "You've got my attention."

"Mother is safe for now. I've spoken with her. She mentioned hearing conversations between Ivan and his father, Javier. She told me Ivan has concerns about drug trafficking that might affect Double Ace. She also mentioned a raid. Am I anywhere close?" He could hear Thad's deep breaths on the other end of the phone.

"Close enough I'm going to make a recommendation. Meet with Gage. He's a straight shooter." Thad chuckled, then cleared his throat. "Well, he can't lie worth shit anyway. Tell him what you told me. You'll learn what you need to know."

"Thanks, brother. I owe you."

"You don't owe me anything, man. But watch your back. I have a feeling whoever is behind your mother's kidnapping is also involved in whatever is going on at Double Ace."

Gage stood on the porch of their beachfront cottage, sipping a cup of coffee as he watched the early morning sun play across the water. Skye still slept inside, needing rest after several rounds of intense lovemaking. A slow grin spread across his face. He'd never been with a woman so honest about her desires, every emotion on display across her beautiful face. She didn't have to tell him how she felt, which scared the hell out of him.

Not because he believed she loved him, but because Gage knew he was falling in love with her.

"Gage?"

Skye walked toward him, a cup of coffee in one hand, her phone in the other. "Kade called me. He wants to speak with you." She held it out to him.

Taking it from her, he leaned down, pressing a kiss to her lips before putting the phone to his ear. "Good morning, Kade. I can't believe you tracked me down on a Sunday."

"Wasn't hard. I heard Skye had flown out of town for the weekend. Figured she'd be coming your way."

"You figured right." Gage slipped an arm around her waist, tucking Skye into his side. "What can I do for you?"

"I wondered if you had time to meet with me tomorrow or Tuesday."

"You're thinking of flying to Houston? Must be serious."

"I'd like to meet in Austin. Early afternoon, if that works for you."

Gage's chest began to tighten, wondering what could be so serious it would bring Kade to Texas to meet with him. And in Austin, not Houston. "Skye flies out at nine. I can be in Austin by noon."

"Make it one. Juan's Casita on Manor Road."

"Are you going to tell me what this is about?" Gage let his arm drop from Skye's waist, turning away.

"I spoke with a mutual friend of ours. Thad Montgomery."

Gage's stomach clenched. "Yeah, I know him."

"He wouldn't tell me anything, except to suggest I talk to you."

"No problem. I'll see you tomorrow at one." He stared at the phone, then handed it back to Skye.

She took it from him, studying his face, unable to miss the lines of concern. "What's going on?"

"You're not flying out tomorrow morning. Instead, we're driving to Austin to meet Kade."

"Why?"

Wrapping an arm around her shoulders, he turned her toward the door. "Let's go inside, sweetheart. There are some things I need to tell you."

Chapter Seventeen

Austin, Texas

"Kade texted. He's at the airport and on his way here." Gage glanced at Skye before sliding his phone into his pocket. The Mexican restaurant held about thirty people, had the standard menu of tacos, enchiladas, burritos, rice, and beans, and seemed to cater to those with little time or who worked close by.

"Do you think Kade has more information than what your friend turned up?" Skye took a chip from the basket, digging into the bowl of guacamole.

"From what Kade said, Thad didn't give him much information, other than recommend he talk to me. Kade's looking for what I told you last night." He picked up a chip, holding it in his hand. "I should've told all of you right away."

Skye shrugged. "I may be wrong, but I'm pretty certain Kade or Matt would've done the same thing. The raid turned up nothing and your files are clean. In my mind, it's not a big deal."

Gage believed Kade would feel differently, especially with the threat to his mother. "Ivan and I thought the same. Plus, we've done our own checks of trucks." Shaking his head, he leaned back in the chair. "I don't know what more we could've done."

Glancing over his shoulder at the sound of the front door opening, he spotted Kade, his expression tense. Standing, he held out his hand.

"Kade."

Clasping the outstretched hand, he looked at Skye. "I thought you were flying back to Crooked Tree this morning."

Lifting her chin, she didn't flinch at his hard glare. "I decided it best to stay here. After all, Double Ace is my account. I need to be in on what's happening, even if it doesn't affect our contracts."

Kade couldn't argue with her. Sitting across from them in the booth, he watched Gage slip an arm around Skye's shoulders. Before he could comment, a young man stopped by their table, taking their order, scribbling it on a small pad of paper.

"How's Reyna doing?"

"Good, Skye. She had a rough few days, but is settling in well. Brooke and I are trying to convince her to stay."

"She can't leave now. I mean, there's still a huge threat in León, isn't there?" She leaned forward, picking up her drink.

"It's more complicated than that." He looked at Gage. "My father and my mother never married. There's some unfinished business between them, which they'll either deal with or not. She wants to be in Fire Mountain, and he wants her there. It doesn't mean there isn't a lot of tension between them."

"Skye told me a little about the relationship. Nothing of that sort is ever easy."

"Hell, no relationship is easy. Regardless, I'd like to see Mother as far away from what's going on in Mexico as possible. She has dual citizenship, so there's no issue on that end." He quieted when the waiter brought their food. "But I didn't fly down here to talk about Mother, although from what I've pieced together so far, she *does* figure into this. Right, Gage?"

Burrito halfway to his mouth, Gage stopped, setting it down without taking a bite. "It's not complicated, and there wasn't any attempt to keep anything important out of your hands."

"Fair enough. Explain it to me." He picked up his carne asada taco, taking a bite, his eyes still focused on Gage.

It didn't take long for him to explain what had transpired over the last few months, including his meetings with Ivan and Ivan's discussion with his family.

"So the first time you noticed something strange was when a truck's log didn't make sense?" Kade asked.

"Right. That was before Matt's wedding, but after he'd started working for you. It happened on more than one occasion, forcing Ivan and me to take a real hard look at the drivers. That's when we first brought Thad into it."

Kade pushed away his empty plate, resting his arms on the table. "You said he used detection dogs each time and came up with nothing."

"The same as recently." Gage rubbed his forehead. "Then the feds raided us. They found nothing, and no deficiencies in any of our paperwork. The thing is, I'm certain something's going on, but can't figure out what it is. After the kidnappings, we're more certain than ever."

"Ivan and Mother said there were no demands, nothing indicating why they were taken."

Leaning forward, Gage placed his arms on the table. "Our stock manager, Eddie Gonzalez, said he got an anonymous phone call the night your mother was abducted. Neither he nor I knew about the kidnapping at that point, so the call seemed meaningless. Now, I'm not so certain."

"What did the caller say?"

"Gonzo said the caller spoke Spanish. Translated, he basically told Gonzo we needed to mind our own business." Gage raked fingers through his hair. "At first, we thought it was a prank call. When we connected the dots and started to check it out, the phone records provided nothing. According to Thad, we came to a dead end."

"Given what you knew, I would've said the same." Kade took a drink of his soda, rolling over the series of events. "Did he call again?"

"No. Could've been a coincidence."

"Do you really believe that, Gage?" Skye spoke for the first time. He'd gone over the same explanation with her the night before, answering her questions, becoming more and more frustrated until they'd finally headed to bed.

He snorted, shaking his head. "No. I think everything I've told you is connected." He sucked in a deep breath, letting it out slowly. "But if not drugs, what?"

Glancing around the restaurant, Kade noticed all the other customers had left. "Money for guns."

Gage's jaw slackened, his eyes wide in surprise.

"I don't understand what you mean, Kade." Skye's comment was no more than a whisper.

"It's simple, honey. The cartels need guns. They get them from people in the States, paying cash. And I mean large amounts of cash." Finishing his drink, he set the empty cup down. "They bring cattle across the border, except the trucks carry more than animals. Packages of money are hidden in the trucks."

"I thought there were x-ray machines that could spot unusual cargo."

"There are, Gage. But the cartels have gotten it down to a science. They use small quantities hidden in the framework of the trucks. Most of the time, the size and placement fool the x-ray machines. Plus, they use numerous trucks to transport the money. My guess is they bring it over with your cattle deliveries and with products for other customers."

"How do the guns get across the border? Doesn't the border patrol check for that type of contraband?" Gage had never thought beyond drugs.

Kade sat back in his chair, crossing his arms. "They break them down, brother."

Gage's expression changed as understanding dawned on him. "Take them apart, ship the pieces in separate trucks."

"Right. Remember, a few strategically placed border patrol and customs agents on the cartel payroll can let a lot of contraband pass by without being discovered. The warning was meant to tell you to stop inspecting the trucks. Who was in charge of that anyway?"

"My stock manager, Gonzo."

"Each time?" Kade dropped his arms, resting them on the table.

"Thad was there with the detection dogs a few times, but the last few were inspected by Gonzo. I did hire four extra men to keep watch on the driver and anyone he brought with him, but the search was solely Gonzo's responsibility."

Skye placed a hand on Gage's arm. "Are you certain Gonzo couldn't be involved?"

He looked at her, his eyes blinking a few times before he shook his head. "No. Absolutely not. He's my top man, helps support his brother's family…" Gage's voice trailed off, his gaze moving away from Skye to focus on the wall behind Kade. "His brother is a retired border patrol agent. From what I know, it was a medical retirement. Gonzo told me he knew just where to look to find contraband." His gaze darted around the room as he tried to come up with a plausible explanation.

Kade stayed silent, letting Gage reach his own conclusions. From being with the DEA, he knew the disillusionment and pain when learning one of your own was a traitor. He'd seen it with another agent and inside the motorcycle gang. In his mind, almost everyone could be bought. You just had to know their price.

"Fuc—" Gage slammed a fist on the table. "Gonzo's involved, isn't he?"

Kade's voice held no emotion when he answered. "That would be my guess, but we can't go accusing him without proof."

"What can we do?" Skye asked, seeing the anguish on Gage's face.

"That's a good question. If it's okay with you, Gage, I'd like to talk to Thad and bring Nesto into this."

"Whatever you need, but I'd like to be a part of it."

"Done." Kade stood. "Let's get out of here and make those calls."

Fire Mountain

"I'll assign someone to watch your mother, then arrange a flight to Houston." Nesto paced outside the ranch house, the phone pressed close to his ear. None of the intelligence he'd gathered indicated the cartel had located Reyna. "Rafe is working out of the house. Trust me, he keeps a close eye on her."

Kade kept the phone on speaker so Gage and Skye could listen and comment. "The sooner the better, bro. We need to get this wrapped up soon."

"Who's going to contact the brothers?" Nesto asked, referring to Heath, Jace, and Rafe.

"I will." Kade planned to call his father first, then go from there.

"And Ivan?"

"Gage will handle that part. I'll arrange a meeting with everyone as soon as you give me details of your flight."

"I'll get on it right now."

Nesto palmed his phone. He'd find someone to watch over Reyna, make a few calls, and hopefully get on a plane within a few hours. The impatience in Kade's voice told him the urgency required to arrange what his friend planned.

Heading inside, he stopped at the sound of another call. Checking the number and not recognizing it, he almost didn't answer, then decided it might be Gage or Skye.

"Salgado." He didn't have much patience as the silence stretched beyond a few seconds. "Speak to me or I'm hanging up."

"Nesto?"

The soft voice had his heart thundering in his chest, his throat swelling, the effort to talk painful.

"Nesto, are you there?"

Fighting the urge to end the call, he hardened his voice. "Yeah, I'm here."

"It's Paige."

One slow breath in, then let it out, he told himself. "I recognize your voice." He didn't know what she wanted, nor did he plan to make it easy for her. It had been months since she'd disappeared, left him without an explanation other than she needed to go home.

"It's been a long time."

Closing his eyes, he fought for patience. "It has. Look, Paige, I'm in the middle of something here. Is there a reason for your call?"

He pictured her brows scrunching together as she bit her lip. It was her go-to expression when confused or stressed. When they'd been together, he'd wrap his arm around her, talk

Paige through whatever weighed on her. Now, all he wanted was for her to spit it out so he could end the call.

"Brooke invited me to Fire Mountain. I didn't—"

"What?" The word was out before he could stop it. As soon as he hung up, he'd track down Brooke to learn what the woman was up to.

"I wondered if she'd mentioned it to you."

"No, she hasn't said a word." He sat down on a nearby bench, rubbing the back of his neck.

"I was afraid of that. Look, I won't come out if it'll bother you."

It irked him she thought he still pined for her, couldn't be around her without missing what they had. "Look, if you want to come to Fire Mountain, go for it. You and I have been through for months. I'll give you your space as long as you do the same for me." He could hear her heavy breathing, the sound of it reminding him of other late night phone calls they used to share. He ignored the pain, the same as he had since she'd walked away.

"She, um…told me about you leaving the marshals and working for the MacLarens. It sounds like a great opportunity. I know you talked about leaving—"

"Yeah, Paige, I remember. Leaving so you and I would have a more stable life. Look, it's over between us, and I'm not in the mood to revisit the past. Make your reservations, come on out, and stay as long as you can before your parents order you home." He winced at what he'd said, then pushed away the guilt. Sometimes, the truth hurt.

"Okay then. I'll confirm with Brooke. It was, um…good talking to you. You know, hearing your voice."

Whatever, he thought, checking his patience once again. "Yeah. Look, I've gotta go."

Hanging up, he struggled to draw in a breath. He stood, fisting his hands on his hips, and stared up at the sky. "Shit," he mumbled, sliding the phone into his pocket.

He'd pushed thoughts of Paige as far out of his mind as possible, moving to another state, finding new friends. His mind wandered to Janie. If she were available, he'd be all over it. But, like him, her heart was still tangled up with someone else.

"Damn." He wanted to shout it. Instead, he tried to rein in his emotions.

"Are you talking to me, Nesto?"

Pivoting on his heel, he came face-to-face with Reyna, amusement on her face. "No, Mama Reyna. I was thinking of something else. Do you need anything?"

She studied him, knowing there was more to it, but letting it go. "Not at all. I needed some fresh air. I wondered, though. Do you think the MacLarens would mind if I took out one of the horses?"

"I don't believe they'd mind at all, as long as someone rides along with you. I'll be out of town for a few days, but I'm sure Annie and Heath, or maybe Rafe would be glad to take a break. From what Kade says, they don't get out on their horses as often as they should."

"Wonderful. I'll go inside and speak with Annie now." She touched his arm, then started to turn away.

"Mama Reyna?"

"Yes?"

"You're going to need to take one of the men with you." He shrugged when he saw her face fall. "Kade will have my head if anything happens to you."

"I understand. Let me speak with Annie. I'm sure she'll find a solution." Her serene smile always warmed his heart, the same as it had all those years ago when life didn't go as planned.

Watching her walk away, Nesto forgot about Paige and her unsettling call for a moment. He knew she and Brooke were good friends. He'd met her after Kade and Brooke got together. The connection had been immediate and strong. They'd fallen in love, talked of marriage and children. Then, one day, she'd walked out of his life.

"I don't have time for this," he mumbled, going into the house and into the study. He had a lot to do before heading to Houston. After Paige's call, he couldn't wait to get away.

Chapter Eighteen

"You don't have to feel obligated to go with me, Rafe. Isn't one of the ranch hands available?" Reyna stood to one side as he led a gentle mare out of her stall. Annie hadn't mentioned Rafe would be the one riding with her. Reyna thought he'd be too busy after taking Nesto to the airport that morning.

Tossing the lead rope over a rail, Rafe crossed his arms, giving her an indulgent smile. "First of all, I don't feel obligated. It's been too long since I've given Blister a good workout, and today's a fine day for it. Second, everyone else has a job to do. I'm your only choice, unless you'd rather wait until later in the week when one of the men is free." Turning back to the mare, he picked up a brush, readying her for the blanket and saddle. "I'm riding out in fifteen minutes, with or without you."

She brushed hair away from her face, biting her lip. "If you're going anyway, I'd love to ride with you."

His choked laugh triggered a reluctant smile from her. "Well, that's real nice of you." Cinching the saddle, he gave Reyna an appraising look, his mind going back many years to a time when conversation came easy for them. Since the day she arrived at the ranch, their conversations had been stilted, clouded by their past mistakes. He wanted that to change.

"Can I do anything to help?" She twisted the brim of her hat in her hands, trying to calm her runaway heart. It hadn't slowed a beat since she'd walked into the barn to find Rafe saddling his horse.

"You can grab bottles of water, maybe a couple energy bars. Do you have a rain slicker? You never know about the weather around here."

Nodding, she started for the house. "I'll be right back."

His shoulders sagged as he blew out a slow breath. Being around her was proving to be more difficult than he'd ever expected. The feelings he thought had died years ago flared to life when he saw her exit the plane, and he hadn't been able to cool the flames since. Rafe wondered if she felt any of the same internal conflicts, if she still held any desire for him at all.

"Hope I didn't take too long."

He chuckled at her attempt to juggle everything in her arms, then hurried to help when bottles slipped to the ground. Brushing off the dirt, he took the rest of what she held, letting his fingers brush across hers, seeing her eyes light up at the brief contact.

"I, uh…better put these away so we can leave. I told Annie you'd be back in time to help with dinner." Ever since his major screw-up when he first saw her helping in the kitchen, he'd tempered his comments, doing his best to think before saying something he'd regret.

Minutes later, she stood next to the mare, preparing to mount.

"Do you remember how we used to do this?" Settling his hands on her waist, he leaned over her shoulder. Inhaling the scent unique to Reyna, he felt her tense, then shiver as his warm breath washed over her cheek. "One, two…" On three, he lifted her, easily setting her atop the saddle. "Let me check the stirrups."

She rested her left boot in the stirrup, then removed it, allowing him to make an adjustment. Once he'd finished with both stirrups, he took the reins, guiding the horse next to Blister.

"He's a magnificent horse, Rafe." Reyna wasn't the best judge of horses, but even she couldn't miss the beautiful lines of the gelding.

Smiling, he ran a hand down Blister's neck. "I've had this ol' boy fourteen years and he's as spry as ever."

The look he gave his horse, the way he stroked his neck, had Reyna wishing for things she knew would never happen. It pained her to accept the truth—Rafe tolerated her for the sake of peace within the family. When the danger ended, she'd return to León. Hoping for anything more would be futile, the same as a little girl's dream of being a princess rescued by a gallant knight. She snickered at the thought, trying to cover the sound with her hand.

"Did you say something?" Rafe climbed into the saddle, glancing at Reyna.

Removing her hand, she changed the subject. "I was just wondering if my horse has a name."

"Annie named her. She's Sugar Foot."

Reyna smiled, leaning forward to stroke the horse's neck. "I'm certain it suits her. Well, are we ready?"

"Anxious, are you?"

Forcing herself to relax, she nodded. "I've been hoping to do this since my first day here."

Slipping on his sunglasses and lowering the hat on his forehead, he sent her a wicked smile. "Then let's get you on the trail."

Houston

Gage took a seat in the borrowed conference room a few miles from Double Ace. Skye, Kade, Nesto, and Thad were deep in conversation about how to proceed. Kade had stayed with Gage the night before, not commenting when Skye automatically walked into Gage's bedroom. She didn't make an issue of it, just hugged her brother and went to bed. It had been quite a while until they'd dropped off to sleep. Shaking his head, he focused on the reason for their meeting.

Clearing his throat, he got everyone's attention. "The way I see it, we need to set up surveillance on at least the next stock delivery." Gage handed out schedules of upcoming deliveries. "Thad, I'd like to hire you to observe the unloading process. We still have the four men you recommended, so you'll have plenty of backup. I'll make certain Gonzo is offsite during the deliveries."

Thad checked the dates. "I can be there. Do any other Double Ace employees help with unloading?"

"Generally, no. Paco may help if he's working that day. He's a college student on a limited work schedule."

"Do you trust him?" Thad set the schedule aside, resting his arms on the table.

"As much as I can trust anyone right now." Gage rubbed the back of his neck, his brows drawing into a frown. "I can't see him involved. Paco is in his early twenties, works hard as one of our stockyard hands. He's not here enough to get involved with whatever is going on, and I doubt the cartels would trust him."

"You'd be surprised who they use for their shipments. If Paco shows up to help, I'll have him stay so as not to raise suspicions. After Gonzo leaves, I'd suggest you spread the word that an associate of Ivan's will be touring the place."

Gage nodded. "I'll have Gonzo visit one of our vendors across town, then make the announcement. He'll be gone all afternoon."

Kade scribbled a few notes, then looked up. "Nesto, I'd like you to follow the truck when it leaves. We've already determined it doesn't go right back across the border. We need to know why."

"No problem."

Gage looked at Skye, then over at Kade. "Will you be staying or flying back to Crooked Tree."

"I'm staying," Skye answered without hesitation. Glancing at Kade, she saw his gaze narrow. "What? I can work from here as well as I can in Crooked Tree."

Kade's mouth drew into a thin line before he shifted to look at Gage. "It's your call as far as who gets involved."

Gage felt cornered into voicing what he wanted instead of what he thought best. Turning toward Skye, his face softened. "I don't want you here for this, Skye. We don't know what we'll find or how it will play out if we rile the wrong people."

"But—"

He held up his hands, stopping her. "Kade, Thad, and Nesto have been trained for this type of work. Neither one of us has any experience for what we're facing. One newbie in the group is already one too many." Reaching over, he took her hand in his. "Go back home, Skye."

She waited a few heartbeats, hoping he'd add that he'd fly up when it was all figured out. When he didn't, she pulled her hand away and looked at the others.

"Do you three honestly believe this is a dangerous situation?"

Kade, Thad, and Nesto each responded with a resounding *yes*.

Thad crossed his arms, resting his back against the chair. "This isn't a joke. It's some serious shit and we need to pay attention to the warnings."

"Skye, we've seen enough of what the cartels do to know they don't play around. What's happening here isn't some game. It's the way they do business." Kade leaned toward her. "They took my mother and Ivan's. The fact they weren't harmed is a mystery and a miracle. I'd bet money a cartel lackey gave the feds enough information to perform the raid at Double Ace. They did this to scare Gage and Ivan—get them to back off from searching the trucks. Their next move won't be so gentle."

For an instant, it seemed Skye wouldn't respond. Then she straightened in her chair, crossing her arms. "I realize this is a dangerous situation and can't be ignored. That's why leaving doesn't seem right. There must be something I can do."

"Skye…" Kade began before Gage held up his hand.

"It's my call, and I say you get on the first plane out of here." The flash of pain crossing Skye's face almost stopped him. Then he thought of how he'd feel if she experienced the same fate as Reyna. "When this meeting is over, we'll pick up your things from my house and I'll take you to the airport." Without waiting for her to reply, Gage turned back to Kade.

Her first instinct was to argue, plead her case for staying. Judging by the expressions on the faces of Nesto, Thad, and Kade, she knew they'd defer to Gage, and he'd already made up his mind. Further argument wouldn't help, and Skye refused to be perceived as a petulant child. Instead, she kept her expression neutral, as if she were agreeing by staying silent. If Mitch or Sean were here, they'd know her silence indicated anything but capitulation. She let the conversation drift around her, appearing disinterested while taking in every word. Gage may have dismissed her, but she was far from walking away.

Fire Mountain

"What do you think?" Rafe reined Blister to a stop at the top of a high hill overlooking the town below.

"It's beautiful. I had no idea the town was so large."

"I forgot you've been stuck on the ranch. We'll have to change that. Tomorrow night, I'll take you to dinner in Fire Mountain. It might surprise you how many good restaurants we have out this way."

For a moment, Reyna couldn't speak, surprised at his invitation. Circumstances had cornered him into riding with her today. It hadn't occurred to her that Rafe might want to spend more time with her. His swings in mood—one moment being civil, the next barely cordial—had her puzzled.

"Reyna? Did you hear me?"

Pushing aside her confusion, she looked at him. "Yes. Having dinner with you tomorrow would be wonderful."

He didn't show his relief, other than to nod. "We'll head west another mile, then stop to stretch. There's a spot I want to show you."

Unaccustomed to being on a horse, her lower back and rear end already ached, both begging for relief. She refused to voice her discomfort. After all, she'd been the one begging for a ride. Concentrating on the scenery, she willed the time to pass quickly.

It took another half an hour to reach the place. As they rounded a bend in the trail, it became apparent why Rafe had wanted to bring her to this spot.

"This is magnificent." Bringing Sugar Foot to a stop, she didn't wait for Rafe as she slid to the ground. A natural spring about twenty yards wide by thirty yards long churned before her, inviting Reyna to kick off her boots and wade in. Surrounded by tall scrub oak and various types of pine, it was the perfect oasis for tired travelers.

"It's one of my favorite places on the ranch."

"We're still on MacLaren property?"

"We've been on MacLaren land since leaving the barn." Rafe did what Reyna had been considering—pulling off his boots and rolling up his jeans. "Care to wade in?"

Not hesitating, she hurried to follow his lead, joining him by the water's edge. "I can't remember the last time I did something like this."

Her bright smile speared right through him. Trying to concentrate on her comment, Rafe resisted the urge to place a hand over his heart. "Wade in the water?"

"Anything spontaneous. Life in my sister-in-law's house is quite structured with many rules. There's little time to just, well…I don't know…be myself."

It felt as if a curtain had been pulled away, revealing a Reyna who'd been relegated to a life far removed from the girl he remembered. Always laughing, impulsive, looking for ways to break the rules, the same as Rafe. At the time, it seemed they'd been made for each other. Until she became pregnant and her family disappeared. Looking at her, regret lanced through him.

"How long has it been since you've done something you truly wanted?"

She shook her head, her eyes not meeting his. "It doesn't matter. I'm here now and intend to enjoy every minute."

Nodding, he held out his hand. "Let's do this together."

Her throat tightened as she looked at his hand. For some reason, she felt taking it would mean more than she wanted it to. Holding it, then letting go would be more difficult than she wanted to accept. Catching her lower lip between her teeth, she took the plunge.

"All right." Slipping her fingers through his, she followed him into the water, shrieking when the ground dropped off, her jeans getting soaked where she'd rolled them up.

"I've got you, Reyna." Rafe held steady as she continued to search for purchase in the sandy bottom. After one more slip, she seemed to find her footing, gracing him with a smile.

Ignoring her soaked jeans, she tightened her grip on his hand and looked around. "This is spectacular. It would be so tempting to hide out here for days…weeks."

"My first year back in Fire Mountain, I rode out with my sleeping bag and enough food for three days. Stayed right over there." He pointed to a spot about five yards away. "Best three days I've had in a long time." Rafe settled his gaze on her. "Until now."

Wondering at the meaning of his words, she searched his face. The years fell away as she saw the same strong features, angular jaw, dark mahogany hair highlighted with a few streaks of silver, and bright green eyes she'd fallen in love with as a girl. The same face she saw in her dreams almost every night for over thirty years. Feeling a tug on her hand, her feet seemed to move without command. Her lips parted as he pulled her close.

"Rafe…" His whispered name fell between a question and a plea.

He didn't respond at first as his fingers grazed down her face, then cupped the back of her neck. "I've wanted to do this from the instant you walked off that plane." Lowering his head, his lips brushed across hers. Pulling away, he looked into her eyes. "If you don't want this…"

Letting go of his hand, she wrapped her arms around his neck, gently tugging him back down. "I've wanted this for a long, long time."

His eyes clouded, the emotion so intense, it almost choked him. "So have I, sweetheart. So have I."

Chapter Nineteen

Houston

Gage picked up Skye's bag, turning from the ticket counter. "Your plane leaves in a little over an hour."

She already knew that. She'd been standing next to him while he checked flights, whipping out his credit card to pay. Skye hadn't expected him to come inside. As naïve as it now seemed, she'd hoped he'd drop her off, allowing her to go ahead with her own plans.

Taking the boarding pass he held out, they walked toward the gate.

"You don't have to go all the way to security. I'm perfectly capable of finding my own way."

Her words were harsher than intended, but justified in her mind. Gage had said no more than ten words to her since leaving the meeting. He'd stayed in the living room while she threw her few belongings into her bag. The ride to the airport had been in strained silence, each glancing at the other every few minutes, neither willing to venture into the gray area between them. Gage had said nothing about seeing her again, nor had he talked about calling her after the current situation at Double Ace was resolved.

This wasn't at all how she thought their weekend together would end. Before the call from Kade, she would have described their time together as idyllic, better than she'd hoped. As hard as she tried, Skye couldn't come up with one thing about Gage she didn't like. Right now, though, she could come up with several. Increasing her pace, she tried to put some distance between them.

"Skye, hold up."

Stopping, she spun around to face him. "Go on back, Gage. I'm perfectly capable of getting on a plane by myself." She started to turn away, stopping when his hand gripped her arm.

"I asked you to wait."

"Fine," she hissed out, her patience growing thin.

Raking a hand through his hair, Gage glanced around as if clearing his head. "Do you think I *want* you to leave?"

Huffing out a breath, she glared at him. "Of course you want me to leave. You're the one who made the decision, drove me to the airport, selected the flight, and paid for it. Geez, Gage, how could I not think you want to get rid of me?"

His eyes darkened, face hardening as he grabbed her hand, pulling her out of the mass of travelers. "I'm not getting rid of you." Gage's nostrils flared as he pieced together how to explain his actions. "Look, the weekend was great."

Throwing up her hands, she rolled her eyes. "Well, I'm glad you think so."

"Dammit, Skye. I'm trying to tell you something." Sucking in a breath, he waited for her to settle down.

Crossing her arms, she nodded. "All right. Tell me."

Lowering his voice, Gage leaned close. "None of us knows what's going on. The only consensus is we're in the middle of something that could be more dangerous than Ivan and I first imagined. I can't have you anywhere near it." He glanced away, his gaze shifting to focus on a spot behind her.

Skye could see his throat work, as if there were more he wanted to say, but didn't know how. Touching his arm, she drew his gaze back to her.

"Why can't I be here? Help me understand." She watched his face cloud over.

"Is it so damn hard to understand?"

Blinking away her confusion, her brows drew together. "Well, yes."

"Ah, hell." Wrapping an arm around her waist, he pulled her close. "I love you, Skye. I don't know how it happened and, God knows, it's not what I planned. Having you anywhere near what's going on doesn't work for me. I need you safe and as far away from this as possible." Waiting, his chest squeezed when she continued to stare, saying nothing. "Don't you have anything to say?"

Licking her lips, she circled her arms around his neck. "Um, could you say the part about loving me again?"

Chuckling, his face softened. "I love you. Is that what you wanted to hear?"

"Oh yeah. That's real good stuff."

"And?" Gage tugged her closer

"Well…"

His lips twitched at the corners, his eyes narrowing. "Are you going to make me drag it out of you?"

"Persuasion would be better," she teased, her eyes twinkling in amusement.

"Oh yeah?" His mouth descended on hers, taking control in an almost brutal kiss, not letting up until she pulled back, gasping for air. Clearing his throat, his voice was thick. "Was that persuasive enough?"

Stroking the back of his neck, her face softened. "You're really good at that, Mr. Templeton."

"How good?"

Giving in, she whispered the words he wanted to hear. "I love you, too, Gage."

"You aren't going to be angry with me for making you leave?" Gage held Skye's hand as they stood outside the security check. If someone hadn't yelled for them to get a room, they might still be wrapped around each other.

"I can't see how being angry with you would help. You already know I don't want to go, but I understand your reasons, even if I don't agree with them."

Gage studied her face. Something was off, but he didn't know what until an idea gripped him. One he didn't like. "You *are* getting on the plane, right?"

She glanced away. "It's what you want."

Holding her chin, he forced her to look at him. "That's not what I asked. You *are* going to board the plane and fly home. Right?"

"That's the plan."

"That's not an answer. Tell me you don't plan to wait until I leave, then catch a cab back to my place." The look on her face, the way her eyes shifted told Gage he'd hit on her plan. "Dammit, Skye. Promise me you *will* get on that plane and you *will* fly home."

"I, um…"

"I'll have your promise on this."

"Or what?"

He let out a frustrated breath. "I have a friend with a basement. No windows, one door, and locks you wouldn't believe."

The air went out of her lungs, her shoulders sagging. "Oh, all right. I'll get on the plane."

"Promise me."

"Geez. Fine. I promise. Are you happy now?"

A slow grin spread over his face. "Yeah, I am." Dropping a quick kiss on her mouth, he squeezed her hand. "It's time to find your gate."

"I know. So you'll call me?"

He brushed a strand of hair off her face, tucking it behind her ear. "Every day. When this is over, you and I are going to take a week away. Somewhere far from family and work. Sound good?"

The excitement his idea created had her heart beating overtime. "You and me alone is a great idea. Where?"

"Anywhere you want, as long as there's privacy. I plan to keep you naked and all to myself for as long as possible." He kissed her again, a little longer.

"Hmmm. Sounds perfect." She let out a breath, gripped the handle of her bag, and stepped away. "I'll call you when I get to Crooked Tree."

Gage nodded. "Be safe, Skye."

I love you, she mouthed, turning away.

He watched until she disappeared through the security section and turned toward her gate, knowing he must look like an idiot standing alone, a crooked grin on his face.

Four years ago, his world fell apart. In the span of seconds, he'd lost his wife, his brother, and a good deal of self-respect. He'd rebuilt his life, believing what he'd created was all he needed to be happy and fulfilled. Skye had shown him how wrong he'd been.

Heading back to his truck, Gage's phone started to ring. He pulled it from his pocket.

"Gage Templeton."

"It's Thad. You need to get to Double Ace right away." The urgency in his voice had Gage's stomach churning.

"What is it?"

"Ivan's missing."

Juarez, Mexico

Ivan's hands were tied to the sides of the wooden chair, a strip of duct tape covering his mouth, the bright lights blinding him. He'd been sitting alone for hours in the concrete room without windows. The one metal door remained closed and locked. A table and chair sat against one wall.

He'd expected to be questioned and beaten, or worse. Instead, no one had appeared. If he had to guess, he'd put money on being in one of the half-finished buildings in Juarez, the twin city to El Paso. Although they were nothing like the twin cities most Americans knew.

El Paso might be a rough border town, the usual drugs and other illegal activities mixed in with a majority of decent citizens and honest businesses, but across the border, Juarez stood as a beacon of corruption, dirty business, and death. Ivan could move within its borders, but he'd never been an actual part of the city.

The door banging open made his head snap up. A large man, different from the two men who'd escorted him by gunpoint from his parking spot at the airport to a plain white van, entered, stopping a few feet away. Ivan guessed him to be close to his age, maybe a few years younger. Crossing his arms, the man stared down at him.

"I trust you've been treated well."

Ivan studied him. Close to six feet tall and two hundred fifty pounds, the man's speech indicated a level of education not common among the cartel community. The fine cut of his clothes, polished shoes, and manicured nails had the hair on Ivan's neck standing on end. This was not one of the bullies hired to force someone to the cartel's will. He guessed him to be several rungs up on the ladder, a man with power who could either save Ivan's life or snub it out with the snap of his fingers.

"You do not recognize me."

His features seemed familiar, yet he knew he'd never met this man. Ivan shook his head.

"Then I will introduce myself. May name is Fernando Santiago. Your uncle, Octavio, is my father."

Ivan's eyes widened, then narrowed as he reassessed the man's features, understanding why he looked familiar.

"I see my father has never mentioned me to you. My brother and I are from a long-term arrangement he had with our mother. It ended when she died years ago, as did the money he gave her each month. He sat us down, telling us if we wanted to continue with the same lifestyle, we would work for him. At the time, the choice seemed simple." A bitter laugh escaped. "You and I are old enough to know nothing is ever so simple."

Reaching down, Fernando gripped an end of the tape, removing it from Ivan's face with one quick tug. Walking to a nearby table, he poured water from a pitcher into a glass, then returned to Ivan.

"You must be thirsty." Fernando held the glass to Ivan's lips, waiting until he'd taken several swallows. "I assume you have questions."

Ivan cleared his throat, grimacing at the tight bonds restraining his hands and arms. "Why am I here?"

Fernando returned the glass to the table, picking up the chair and moving to within a couple feet of Ivan. Sitting down, he leaned forward, resting his arms on his legs. "It is a good question. My men are the ones who took your mother and Javier's sister."

"You took Mother? Why?"

"As a warning. Unfortunately, the message did not get through to you or *Uncle Javier*." Sarcasm dripped from his voice at the mention of Ivan's father. "I trust they told you they were treated well."

Ivan found it hard to squelch the anger burning in his gut. "If by well you mean they weren't harmed, then yes. Women being taken and held hostage is not an honorable action."

Fernando shrugged. "Perhaps not. I no longer worry about such things as honor."

Ivan ignored the bile building in his throat, forcing himself to concentrate on more important questions. "What message did you expect to send by scaring two innocent women?"

"Innocent? No one is innocent in this. But that isn't important right now. What is important is for you and your man, Templeton, to stop searching trucks. You are to unload the cattle, then let the trucks go on their way. It is a simple request, one that will cause no harm to anyone."

Ivan couldn't stop his incredulous response. "Drugs cause no harm?"

Fernando reared his head back and laughed. Crossing his arms, he settled back in the chair. "Father told me how naïve you are. I should have expected your answer. It is business, Ivan. Nothing more."

"Surely you cannot be serious."

"Oh, but I am. Supply and demand. Our business is to supply what people want. We care not what the product is, as long as someone is willing to pay for it. Money is what matters. The sooner you understand that simple concept, the sooner you will be back in Houston, talking to Templeton."

"So we were not wrong. You *are* bringing drugs into the U.S."

"The product does not matter. It is about demand and supply. Sometimes drugs, sometimes something else. What you must understand is to ignore everything other than the cattle. You do that, and no one will get hurt." Fernando stood, glaring down at Ivan, his voice hard and cold. "There will be no more warnings. This is a courtesy to you, my cousin. If you do not do as I ask, next time, someone you love will be delivered to you in pieces. Am I clear?"

Ivan reared back as if he'd been hit. The thought of his mother, father, or someone else being tortured and killed was a powerful weapon, and Fernando wielded it well.

He'd worked hard to stay away from the cartels and their criminal activities. It was one reason he'd never married. Those with a wife and children were vulnerable to the threats being delivered to him now. Still, his mother and others were in danger if Fernando decided to carry out his threats. Looking at him, Ivan had no doubt the man wouldn't feel any remorse about killing those who stood in his way.

Ivan needed time. He could think of a solution later. Right now, he had to get back to the U.S. and meet with Gage.

"You'll leave us alone as long we stop checking the trucks after the cattle are unloaded?"

Fernando nodded. "That is correct."

"And you'll release me?"

"My men will release you once I leave."

"Then I will do as you ask." Ivan doubted Fernando would simply take his word. If anyone at Double Ace did anything other than stand aside as the cattle were off-loaded, there would be retribution, swift and unyielding.

"That is a wise decision. I will let my men know." Without another word, Fernando turned on his heel and left the room, the outside lock clicking into place.

Ivan let out a breath, wondering how long it would be before someone came in to cut his bindings and take him to safety. Minutes passed before he heard the lock release. The two men who'd abducted him walked in, one holding a knife.

For an instant, Ivan wondered if Fernando had been truthful about letting him go. Then the man bent down, cutting the ties and releasing Ivan's arms. Before he had a chance to stand, a powerful blow landed on the back of his head, spinning him into a world of darkness.

Chapter Twenty

Houston

Dashing through the front door, Gage didn't stop to speak with Daria as he placed his hand on the identity pad, then bounded upstairs and into his office. He stopped short, seeing the grim look on the faces of Kade, Thad, and Nesto.

"Have we heard anything about Ivan?"

Thad stood and walked over to him. "He was found near the border. Badly beaten, but alive."

Gage's jaw tightened, fury choking him, making it difficult to speak. "Where is he?"

Kade came up next to him, placing a hand on Gage's shoulder. "They took him to an emergency clinic, then transferred him to University Hospital. Nesto has a buddy at the marshal service in El Paso. He's the one who cut through the bull and got the information to us."

Nesto sat at the desk, placing the handset down after finishing a call. "Rafe's going to set up additional security at the ranch. The same with Matt in Cold Creek. With Kade down here, Mitch MacLaren has been called back to Crooked Tree. He'll be hiring some extra people to keep watch. We still believe it's doubtful they've connected the Santiago family to the MacLarens. We're just being careful."

Gage's eyes widened, his gaze shooting to Kade. "Skye is on a plane to Crooked Tree."

"Give me the flight information and I'll have someone meet her." Kade pulled out his phone as Gage gave him the airline, arrival time, and flight number, then called the office in Montana.

"I need to get to El Paso." Gage started to call the airport.

"Hold on. Daria called his office in El Paso. They're sending Ivan's plane here and will fly you back." Thad pulled out his keys. "I'll drive you to the airport. Grab anything you need and we'll leave."

Gage's mind whirled at all that had happened, the full impact still not quite hitting him. "What about our plans?"

Kade picked up his notes. "Assuming they stay on schedule, the next truck doesn't arrive until tomorrow. If Ivan is coherent and able to talk, it's important to find out what happened, if they gave him a message or told him what would come next. Right now, the authorities are calling it a random beating and robbery. They aren't looking at the cartels, at least that's what Nesto's contact says. Thad and I are working our contacts in the DEA to see if there's any chatter. So far, nothing."

Nesto leaned back in his chair, crossing his arms. "If you aren't back by the time the truck arrives tomorrow, we'll go forward with what we planned—search the truck, then follow it."

Gage looked at each of them, shaking his head. "This isn't your fight. I can't ask you to go through with this unless I'm here."

Nesto grinned. "You aren't asking us, bro. We've already agreed to do it."

"Get out of here, Gage." Kade slid into a chair. "We need to know what happened to Ivan and we'll only get that information from you."

University Hospital, El Paso

They looked nothing alike, yet no one questioned Gage when he arrived to see his *brother*, Ivan Santiago. What did surprise him was to walk into the room and see Ivan awake and sitting up, his face covered in bruises, his nose taped, indicating it had been broken. Unable to hide his reaction, Gage stepped next to the bed.

"Do I look that bad?" Ivan mumbled through cut and swollen lips.

"I've seen worse on the rodeo circuit. I have to say, Ivan, you're right up there with the best of them." He grabbed a chair, pulling it up to the bed. The moment he saw Ivan, Gage felt as if he'd been jabbed in the stomach. It went well beyond what he'd ever seen before. "Can I get you anything?"

"No. The doctors and nurses are doing everything they can. My father should be arriving soon." Ivan stopped to take a breath, his face showing the pain he felt with each movement.

Gage leaned forward. "You don't need to talk now."

Ivan shook his head. "You must hear…" His voice trailed off, his eyes closing and body going still.

"It's the pain meds." Gage turned to see a nurse standing in the doorway. She took a step forward. "He'll be out for quite a while. You're welcome to wait here, or go to the cafeteria."

"How long before he wakes up?"

"It could be several hours. He took quite a beating and he needs all the rest he can get to heal properly." Walking past him, she checked the monitors.

Gage stood, setting the chair back against a wall. "I could use some coffee."

"The cafeteria is on the main floor. Just take the elevator and follow the signs."

He pulled his phone out, knowing he had little to report to the others. It would be several hours before Ivan would be lucid enough to talk. By then, Ivan's father would be there.

Gage decided to get his coffee, call the others, then wait for Javier to arrive, hoping the senior Santiago didn't prevent him from speaking to Ivan.

Houston

The following morning, Kade stood by the office window, looking out onto the stockyard. "We're going to have to make a decision soon. The truck arrives in less than two hours."

"It's hard to understand why Javier would prevent Gage from speaking to Ivan." Thad pinched the bridge of his nose. The three had taken a few hours to sleep, then reconvened at Double Ace, waiting for any news from Gage.

Nesto paced to the window, standing next to Kade. "It could be nothing more than concern for his son's recovery. From what Gage said, Ivan's in pretty bad shape."

"Or Javier may want to be the first to hear what Ivan has to say." Kade still held out hope Gage would get to Ivan before they had to make a decision to go or stand down.

It had been a tough sell to get the DEA to go along with the scant amount of information provided. Fortunately, between Kade and Thad, they still had enough credibility within the agency to get a plan moving on short notice. The impromptu meeting with the local DEA had gone into the early hours of the morning.

Even though they didn't know if the contraband would be drugs, money, or something else, by the time they broke to get some sleep, the ASAC, Assistant Special Agent in Charge, Mike Bonner, had given his support. With timing so critical, Bonner made a decision to go forward, muttering a curse, wishing his boss weren't going into surgery that morning. The downside was he couldn't pull together more than a few men to help track the truck after it left Double Ace.

Kade checked his watch. They had ten minutes before he had to confirm the mission or call it off. Hearing his phone, he slid it from his pocket, answering it before the second ring.

"Yeah, Gage. Have you spoken with Ivan?" He touched the speaker button, setting the phone on the desk.

"No, and I've no idea when Javier will let me see him." Gage's frustration couldn't be missed. "They only allow one person in the room at a time, so I can't tell you what's going on."

"We need to go with the plan," Thad interjected.

Kade looked at Nesto. "Your thoughts?"

"Everyone is in place. I say we go."

"Gage, the truck will be here in a little over an hour. At this point, we want to go with the plan. If you *do* get anything from Ivan, call me right away."

"Wish I had more for you, Kade. I'm stuck until Javier allows access to Ivan."

"You're doing your best, man. We'll be in touch." Kade hung up, then grabbed the phone off the desk and called Mike Bonner. "We're on."

El Paso

Leaving the cafeteria, Gage held another cup of coffee in one hand, his phone in the other as he stepped into the elevator. He'd done his best to doze in a chair outside Ivan's room, never getting more than thirty minutes sleep before some unwelcome hospital noise woke him. Caffeine and sugar were all that kept him awake.

Walking toward Ivan's room, a rush of disappointment flooded him when he saw the door closed. Dialing Skye's number, he settled into the chair and leaned back.

"Hey, Skye. It's me." They'd talked several times since she'd arrived in Crooked Tree. He found hearing her voice wasn't enough.

"Hold on a minute, Gage, while I close my door." He could hear a chair move and a door shut. "How's Ivan doing?"

He brought her up to speed, holding nothing back, including his level of frustration.

"What has Kade decided?"

"They're going to search the truck, then follow it. It may be a total waste of time." Gage set the coffee cup on the floor, moving the phone to his other ear.

"Or they could be walking into a real bad situation."

Gage blew out a breath. "Yeah, I know. I hate they're putting themselves in possible danger and I'm not even there. It's not right."

"How many times have you been in a situation like the one going on now?"

"Never," he snorted.

"This isn't new for Kade, Thad, or Nesto. And all three were in the military."

"I understand what you're saying. Still, I'm the one in charge of the Houston office, and I'm stuck in El Paso. Javier is stopping me from talking to Ivan. It's a powerless feeling."

"Mr. Templeton?"

"Hold on, Skye." Gage looked up to see the nurse standing before him.

"Mr. Santiago is awake and has asked for you."

"Skye, I've got to go. I'll call you later."

Javier stepped out into the hall, moving aside so Gage could enter. Ivan's father looked as if he'd aged ten years.

"How is he, Mr. Santiago?"

"Ivan is healing, Gage." Javier scrubbed a hand down his face, looking over his shoulder and into the room. "He asked for you. Do not let him get too upset."

"Yes, sir. Do you know what he wants to tell me?"

"I do. But my son should be the one to tell you. I'm sure you'll have questions." Javier walked away, his step not as imposing as Gage remembered.

Houston

"Put the phone down."

Kade, his voice hard and commanding, came up behind the man holding the phone to his ear.

"I, uh…was just calling home." The man's gaze darted from Kade to the men standing around the truck, then to the driver and his partner.

"Give me the phone." Kade held out his hand. He glanced at the number called, knowing he wouldn't recognize it. He'd seen the man make the call. By the time Kade had gotten to him, less than a minute had passed, not much time to notify someone of what was happening.

"It's nothing. I was just making a quick call." He wouldn't meet Kade's eyes.

"For your sake, I hope you're telling me the truth. Come with me, and don't even consider running." He let the man pass by, then followed him to the truck where Thad and Nesto were jumping to the ground, having finished their inspection.

Thad wiped his hands down his jeans, settling his sunglasses back on his face. "What's going on?"

"He was making a call while you and Nesto were inside." Kade handed the phone to Thad while Nesto went to speak with the driver. "Less than a minute passed before I could get to him. It may be nothing, but I can't trust any of Gage's employees right now."

Thad frowned as he looked at the number. "I don't recognize the number. That doesn't mean anything."

The employee looked at Thad, doing his best to hide his fear. "It is nothing. I called a friend of mine."

"Thad, take care of this guy while I talk with Nesto." Kade motioned Nesto to a spot several yards away, his voice low as he explained what happened.

Crossing his arms, Nesto looked behind him at the employee, who appeared ready to bolt, then turned back to Kade. "We don't have time for this. The driver said he's expected to leave within the next few minutes to keep his schedule. I say we secure the employee and toss him into the trunk of my car. The DEA can speak to him when we're done."

"What's your gut telling you?" Kade asked.

Nesto placed a hand on his stomach. "My gut feels like a jackhammer is going off inside it. I'd bet a year's pay they have money tucked away inside the frame of the truck. The telltale signs are there, but we won't know until we tear it apart."

"Tearing it apart will only get us the driver. The truck needs to go to the next destination so the feds can make a bust. They want more than a couple low-level transporters."

"Give me time to secure the guy in my car before you let the truck leave."

Fifteen minutes later, Kade motioned the driver to head out. Thad already sat in his truck, ready to follow. The same with Nesto in his car. Kade signaled Thad to go ahead, then hurried to his car. They expected the DEA agents to meet up with them within a few blocks of Double Ace, tagging each other while following the truck so as not to raise suspicion.

Starting the engine, Kade felt the familiar rush he got with each raid he used to make before he retired. He couldn't stop the thrill running through him or the excitement of being a part of something he used to live and breathe.

El Paso

Gage paced back and forth, his mind reeling with the threats Fernando Santiago had made against his own family.

"He never mentioned anyone other than your family and friends, correct?"

Ivan nodded, closing his eyes as pain rocketed through him. "That is what I remember. But, as Uncle Octavio's son, he is certain to know of Aunt Reyna's connection to the MacLarens."

Which meant he could know about all the MacLarens, including Skye. "And you agreed to stop the searches?"

"I gave the impression we would stop, yes. At the time, he had agreed to release me, which he did." Ivan's face contorted in pain when he choked out a laugh, his broken ribs protesting any movement. "Fernando's word is not to be trusted. My father and I spoke. He does not believe any of us are safe, even if we stop the searches."

"Octavio is his brother. Can't your father reason with him?"

Ivan glanced at the door, making certain it was closed. "My father is in great distress. He did not know his brother had become entangled with the Montalvo-Ortiz cartel. Uncle Stefan swears he knew nothing of Octavio's change in allegiance." Ivan closed his eyes, taking in a slow breath. "My father does not believe him. He has doubled the guards at his home in León, added several more bodyguards, and told my mother she will not be coming home for a while. He has also called Rafe MacLaren."

Gage's chest tightened. He needed to call Skye, tell her of the danger. He thought of Kade, Thad, and Nesto. If all had gone as planned, they were already in the middle of the search, maybe even following the truck at that very moment.

"I've got to call Kade." Pulling out his phone, he dashed out of the room, passing Javier without stopping.

Kade, Thad, and Nesto parked two blocks away from where the DEA surrounded an industrial complex on the south side of the city. Bonner ordered them to stay back, allowing his men to do their job. Their compliance lasted until the man jogged out of sight. Hovering close to the back of a building across the street, they now had an excellent view.

The truck that had left Double Ace parked next to five similar haulers. What surprised everyone was the apparent lack of security.

Nesto had tried to hand off the man secured in the trunk of his car to Bonner. The lead agent had taken a look at the man, asking them to continue holding him. The three were qualified to interrogate him further, find out if he was involved, but that wasn't their role. He now sat in the back of Nesto's car, where he'd stay until the results of the raid were known.

"There they go." Thad stood in plain sight, unconcerned about anyone spotting him. "Wish I could be with them."

The words were barely out of Thad's mouth when a barrage of gunfire ripped through the morning air, followed by shouts and more gunfire. Without warning, the attack on the agents came from the men working inside the trucks and the warehouse.

Without taking time to check with each other, Kade, Thad, and Nesto drew their weapons and dashed across the street.

Compared to the DEA agents, they were ill-prepared to take fire.

"We've got this, Montgomery." Bonner motioned them to stay back. "I need you behind cover."

"He's right. It's their job now." Kade's eyes narrowed, his senses on alert as they watched the scene play out from behind a row of cars.

The fighting continued for another few minutes before the area went silent.

"Over there." Thad pointed to the side of the building. Two agents held their weapons on a group of men walking in front of them with their hands up.

"Do you recognize any of them?" Nesto asked Thad.

"I can't get a good look at their faces. The way Bonner's staring at them, I'd bet money he recognizes at least one. Looks like he's waving us over."

"I'm going to get the guy in my car. It's time to turn him over and let them decide if he's worth holding." Nesto jogged away in the opposite direction as Thad and Kade headed toward Bonner.

A few minutes later, Nesto returned with the man, stopping next to Bonner. "He may or may not be involved. He pulled out his phone and made a call the instant we started searching the truck back at the yard. We thought it best to bring him along, have you decide if he's someone of interest."

The instant the man caught sight of the other men in custody, he jerked hard, trying to get away. Slender and several inches shorter than Nesto, his efforts soon became futile.

Bonner glared at him. "What's your name?" The man shook his head, muttering under his breath. "You can tell me your name now or wait until we get you back to headquarters. Doesn't matter to me."

Lifting his head, his body shook as his gaze darted between the men in custody and the agents.

Nesto loosened his grip on the man's arms. "Give him your name, buddy. Maybe we can clear this up now and you can go home."

He shook his head, muttering what sounded like a prayer, and looked at Nesto. "It is too late for me. If those men don't kill me," he choked out, glancing at those in custody, "my uncle will."

Kade and Thad stepped closer, taking a better look at the young man.

"Just who is your uncle?" Kade's stomach clenched, his instincts telling him he wouldn't like the answer.

"I'm Paco Gonzalez. My uncle Gonzo is the stock manager."

Chapter Twenty-One

Gage leaned against the wall, his arms crossed, compassion gripping him as Kade spoke with Gonzo. Paco had been firm about his uncle's innocence when he explained his part in helping the cartel. The instant he'd given his brief confession, Bonner had placed him in custody, whisking Paco off with the others they'd captured in the raid.

Disbelief, pain, and anger crossed Gonzo's face as he listened to the events. Gage felt a small measure of guilt at suspecting his stock manager of working with the cartel, sending him offsite for meetings while Kade, Nesto, and Thad took part in the raid. Knowing his nephew, a young man with such promise, had been the inside contact for the Montalvo-Ortiz cartel provided Gage with no sense of relief. He'd been as stunned as Gonzo to learn of Paco's involvement.

"I don't know what to think. My brother will be devastated." Gonzo dragged a shaky hand down his face. Gage had never seen him look so defeated. Pushing away from the wall, he took a few steps forward.

"I've talked to Ivan. He's going to have his U.S. attorney meet with Paco."

Gonzo's eyes widened at Gage's words, then narrowed in disbelief. "Why would he do that? Paco admitted to working with the cartel."

"Bonner called me an hour ago," Thad interjected, leaning forward in his seat across the room. "He says there may be more to Paco's story than he first thought. Without saying as much, he suggested we get a lawyer involved."

Nesto shook his head. "I still can't believe he'd suggest that. It's usually the last move they want to see."

"I agree, but there are extenuating circumstances. Bonner and I were pretty tight when we were both new to the agency. Also, we led him to what he believes is going to be a solid bust. He felt he owed us."

Gonzo rubbed his hands on his pants, a nervous gesture Gage had seen once or twice before. "Did he give you any other information?"

"Sorry, man." Thad shook his head. "We were lucky to get what he provided. Ivan's attorney will be able to give you details. Maybe Paco might be in a position to arrange a plea bargain for testifying against the others."

"And the MacLarens?" Gage asked. "Does Bonner see retaliation?"

Kade joined the conversation. "In my experience, the cartel won't normally come after someone in the States who they don't see as a direct threat. My mother and the other MacLarens know nothing of the people or operations within the cartel. That doesn't mean we shouldn't continue to be vigilant and take precautions. The cartel's first move will be to set up alternative lines of entry so more trucks can move across the border. They won't stay out of action long."

Thad crossed his arms, his expression full of disgust. "They'll be back in business within a week. It's a cycle hard to obliterate. Where there's demand, there's money to be made, and the cartels are masters at making money."

"I agree with Kade and Thad. Still, I'd recommend we keep security boosted a little longer. At least until we know more about Paco's circumstances and any possible retaliation." Nesto looked at Gonzo. "Your family may be in more danger than anyone."

"We have him covered." Gage leaned against his desk. "Ivan has agreed to keep on the four men we hired at Thad's suggestion, plus provide protection for Gonzo's family as long as necessary."

Standing, Gonzo stared at the ground, then lifted his gaze to meet Gage's. "He is already doing enough. I have a large family, and we're used to watching out for each other. Asking his attorney to meet with Paco is enough."

"Are you sure? Ivan made the offer."

"No, Gage, I cannot accept the protection. Tell him thank you, but my family will be fine on its own." Gonzo moved to the door, resting his hand on the knob, letting out a slow breath. "I can never thank all of you enough. I know this had to be hard, learning of Paco's involvement. Still, you have helped my family. I'll never be able to repay you."

Gage moved to him, placing a hand on his shoulder. "There will be no talk of repayment. We're glad to do what we can."

Fire Mountain

Reyna hung up the phone, her features drawn. The last few days, her life had gone so well, better than she'd ever dreamed. The message Kade passed along caused a shadow to obscure the joy she'd been experiencing.

"Are you all right?"

She felt Rafe's hand on her shoulder, the heat radiating through her blouse. Never had she believed the love from her past would reclaim her, offering a future she thought had long ago died. Their ride across the ranch and time at the springs had been a turning point for each of them. As corny as it sounded, she'd been swept away by the same man who'd first captured her heart, making her feel as if she were still seventeen. Reyna didn't want reality crashing down on them right now.

Placing her hand over Rafe's, she turned toward him. "That was Kade. The DEA raided a warehouse outside of Houston. He tried not to alarm me, assuring me it all ended well, but said the security at the ranch would need to continue." Meeting Rafe's gaze, she wrapped her arms around him. "He wants you to call him."

"He wasn't more specific?" He kissed her forehead, then stroked a hand down the back of her head.

"He said something about several loose ends. That's why he wants to talk to you."

Keeping one arm around her, he palmed his phone, glancing at the screen. "Looks like he tried calling me several times. I don't know *how* I could've missed them." His eyes danced in merriment.

They'd spent most of the day in bed, ignoring everything else around them. He'd rented a quaint cabin across town from the ranch, giving them privacy and time to sort out what was happening between them. Relief had settled over him when neither Heath nor Annie had asked specifics when told he and Reyna would be gone for a few days. Their time together had turned into some of the best days of his life, and he suspected Reyna felt the same.

"I'd better call him back."

"You go ahead. I need to shower before we leave for dinner." She leaned up, brushing a kiss across his lips.

Watching her walk into the bath, he felt a joy so strong, it was like a physical presence enveloping him. Placing one hand against his chest, he sucked in a deep breath, letting it out slowly. When the door closed behind her, he punched in Kade's number.

Ten minutes later, he hung up as the bathroom door opened, his happiness now tempered with concern for Reyna and the rest of the family.

Her hair still wrapped in a towel, she stepped up to him, placing a hand on his chest. Looking up, her breath caught at the worry on his face.

"What is it?"

He didn't answer right away. Instead, Rafe wrapped an arm around her waist, drawing her tight against him.

"You'll need to stay in Fire Mountain much longer than we first thought."

His words sent a chill through her. Not so much because she wanted to leave, but because she didn't. They hadn't spoken of a future, yet the last few days had given her hope something permanent might be growing between them. The disappointment in his voice made her think she'd totally misjudged his desire for her to stay. Pushing away, she crossed her arms, preparing for a conversation she'd hoped they would never have.

"If Kade and Ivan think I'm still in danger, I'll leave. There is no point putting you or your family at risk any longer."

Turning, she made it two steps away before a strong hand grabbed her arm, spinning her around. Dragging her to him, Rafe's cold stare cut right through her.

"You aren't going anywhere."

She tugged, but couldn't break his hold. "You said I *need* to stay longer, as if my being here is a burden. I refuse to be an inconvenience to you, Annie, or Heath. Our time together has been wonderful, Rafe, but…" Her voice weakened, her throat thick with emotion.

"What the hell are you talking about, Reyna? You're anything but an inconvenience." Dropping her arm, he turned, pacing a few feet away, then spun around, fingers pinching the bridge of his nose. "Our time together has been a lot more than wonderful…at least to me."

Her face softened, then clouded with confusion. "But you sounded so frustrated with the possibility of me needing to stay longer."

Walking up to her, he placed his hands on her shoulders, then used a finger to lift her chin up.

"What you heard in my voice was frustration that you may still be in danger. I'd hoped what transpired in Houston would end the threat." He caressed her cheek with his fingers. "Kade still has concerns. He asked that I stay close to you." Placing a kiss on her lips, he grinned. "That is no burden at all."

Taking her hand, Rafe sat down on the bed, settling her across his lap. His heart beat in rhythm to the dread building inside him. He couldn't have Reyna doubting him. Reaching to his side, he opened the drawer in the bedside table, clutching a small velvet bag, never dropping his gaze from hers.

"I love you, Reyna. If I have my way, you'll never leave."

Resting her forehead against his, she breathed out a relieved sigh. "I love you, too, Rafe. I've never loved another man. Only you."

"Then marry me, sweetheart. Stay here forever."

Pulling back, her eyes registered surprise before tears began to pool and a smile formed on her lips. Catching a bead of moisture as it descended down her cheek, he chuckled.

"Is this a happy or sad tear?"

Wrapping her arms around his neck, she leaned back, radiance replacing shock. "It's good. Very good."

"Does that mean you'll marry me?"

Nodding, she let her joyful tears continue. "Yes. There's nothing I want more."

Crooked Tree

Gage walked out of the terminal to the sight of a clear, cloudless sky, and a beautiful woman running toward him. Dropping his bag, he held his arms wide, catching Skye as she jumped into them.

"I missed you." Her mouth captured his, not allowing time for a response.

Chuckling, he set her down. "I missed you, too." Looking behind her, he spotted her truck next to the curb. Picking up his bag, he placed a possessive arm around her and walked toward the truck. "I don't care where we go as long as it's just the two of us."

"Good, because I shooed Sam and Rhett out of the house for the next couple days. It's just you and me, cowboy."

Climbing into the passenger seat, he threw back his head and laughed. "I sure would've liked to have heard their comments."

Sliding into the driver's seat, she started the engine, then glanced at him. "Seems they both already figured it out. They were more than happy to give us some privacy."

"Smart kids. How's she doing?"

"Pretty much healed from the accident. Ready to get back on her horse and practice. Tucker's helped out a lot."

His brows knit together. "Tucker? The VP at Maverick West who MacLaren and Double Ace are working with on a joint branding program?"

"One and the same. They've been friends since college. You sure I never mentioned the connection?" She turned into her driveway, seeing the parking area in front of the house empty. Her hands gripped the steering wheel tighter as she let out a shaky breath, her chest constricting.

"Pretty sure I would've remembered." Gage watched the knuckles on her hands turn white as her grip intensified. "Are you all right?"

Turning off the engine, she sat back against the seat, continuing to stare straight ahead. "Fine."

His eyes narrowed as he studied her face. Getting out of the truck, he stepped around to her side, opening the door. "Skye, what's going on?"

Moistening her lips, she turned to face him. "I, um…just…"

"Just what, sweetheart?" Moving closer, Gage took her hands in his. "You're freezing." He began rubbing them between his, worry etched on his face. As they began to warm, he placed a finger under her chin, lifting her gaze to meet his. "Tell me what's going on."

Shaking her head, she let out an unsteady laugh. "It seems I was more worried about you than I thought."

Relief washed over him as he took her in his arms and lifted her from the truck, cradling her against his chest. "I'm here and safe. Nothing happened to me, and nothing's *going* to happen to me, or to you. As far as I'm concerned, it's over." Brushing a kiss across her lips, he walked to the house, pushing open the door. "Guess you're just going to have to get used to having me around."

"Matt and Cassie announced they're pregnant." Skye forked another mouthful of salad, shifting on the bed where they held an impromptu picnic. "Everyone's thrilled, especially Heath and Annie. Oh, and here's some more news. Trey and Jesse are getting out of the Navy and coming home."

Gage swallowed the last bite of his sandwich, following it with a gulp of beer. "Who are Trey and Jesse?"

Skye shrugged. "Trey is Heath's son. He and his wife, Jesse, met while at the Naval Academy, became pilots, married, and are now eligible for discharge. Heath thought they'd stay in, but he got a call a few days ago that they're coming home. Oh, and they have a son, Trevor." Reaching for her t-shirt, she stopped when Gage's hand covered hers.

"No, you don't. I've plans for you after we eat." Picking up a corn chip, he took a bite. "Trey must be older than Cassie."

"He is. I've only met him a couple times, but he seems great. And Trevor is so cute. A mini-Trey."

Gage snorted. "A mini-Trey, huh?" Picking up the chip bag, he set it aside. "Any other MacLarens I need to know about?"

"You already know about the ones in Texas. There are a few in California, but we'll get to those another time." Finishing her salad, she tossed the paper plate in the trash, then squealed when Gage grabbed her around the waist, settling her on her back.

Stretching out on top of her, he trapped her hands above her head, his mouth claiming hers. After a few heated minutes, he raised his head, resting his forehead against hers.

"Marry me, Skye."

Her body jerked under him as her eyes flew open, her jaw dropping. "What?"

"Hold on a minute and don't move." He grabbed his phone and opened the camera app.

She swatted his hand, pushing the phone out of the way. "Don't even think of it."

"But the look on your face…" He started to laugh, then sobered. "So what will it be, Miss MacLaren? Marry me, or keep up this long distance lust affair?"

Pulling her hands free of his grip, she cupped his face. "I prefer to think of it as a long-term love affair."

"Then let's make it official. Marry me."

Kissing him, she smiled. "I can't think of a reason not to."

Epilogue

Fire Mountain

Birdseed flew through the air, the music played, and the newly married couple passed between a crowd of family and friends. Coming to a halt next to Kade, Rafe held out his hand, his arm firmly around Reyna, his new bride.

Kade gripped his father's hand, then pulled him into a hug. "I'm happy for you, Pops."

Rafe's eyes widened marginally as he slapped his son on the back, doing his best to hide the moisture in his eyes. Kade had always refused to call him anything except Rafe. They'd turned a corner, and all because Reyna had come back into his life. Dropping his arms, he stepped aside to let Kade embrace his mother, his gaze settling on his son, Mitch, who talked to Gage a few feet away.

"Guess you're next." Mitch clasped Gage on the shoulder.

Gage tightened his grip on Skye's hand. The night before, they'd announced their plans to marry, stunning everyone except Kade. The peace and happiness Skye brought into his life had been unexpected, especially given the way his last marriage ended. The thought made him think of Brent. He still hadn't returned his call. Maybe be would before the wedding.

Gage sighed. "Your sister wants a big wedding. Me? I just want to get it over with."

"I'm with you, brother. Dana and I snuck off, then had a reception. As far as I'm concerned, it's the only way to end your bachelor status." Mitch turned at the sound of the band tuning up, Kade's voice coming over the microphone.

"It seems this is the weekend for announcements." He tugged Brooke next to him. "Looks like the MacLarens are going to be adding to the clan in rapid succession." He handed the mic to Brooke, a broad smile breaking across her face as she bounced on the balls of her feet.

"I'm pregnant!"

Applause, whoops, and shouts of congratulations rang out as Reyna and Rafe walked up to embrace them.

Trey MacLaren draped an arm across Jesse's shoulders, tugging her to him, whispering in her ear. "Should we wait to make our announcement?"

Jesse placed a hand on her stomach, still flat after two months. "I think you should just go for it, MacLaren."

"Yes, ma'am." Taking her hand, Trey walked up to Kade, a sly grin on his face.

"You, too?" Kade asked, handing him the mic.

"Afraid so." Trey's broad smile revealed his true feelings. "Might as well get it done now."

Fifteen minutes later, everyone toasted the bride and groom, as well as those adding to the family. As the music started, Rafe escorted Reyna to the temporary dance floor, swaying to the sound of their favorite song from years ago.

"I hear you and my cousin are getting married."

Gage turned at the sound of the familiar drawl. "Nicole. Or should I call you Nikki?"

"Either is fine. A small world, isn't it, you knowing my family?" She snorted out a laugh. "The fact is, you probably know them a lot better than me."

"Maybe so, but you can change that." Skye slipped her hand into Gage's. "Come for a visit anytime. You could even talk to the brothers about a job."

Nikki smiled. "I'd like that, although I'm not so sure my folks would appreciate me moving out of Texas." Sipping her drink, she glanced around at the large number of people, her gaze landing on a tall man with broad shoulders, dark close-cropped hair, and stern features standing a few yards away. "Is that a MacLaren?"

Skye followed Nikki's gaze. "No. That's Ernesto Salgado. He heads up security at all the MacLaren companies and is a long-time friend of Kade's. Want me to introduce you?"

Nikki shook her head. "Not now. I'll go up to him later and introduce myself. I'm still trying to sort out who's who." She watched as Kade moved up alongside Nesto, handing him a drink, observing their easy comradery.

"You okay with all of this, man?" Nesto sipped the whiskey, never letting his eyes settle on one place for long. He couldn't let himself forget the recent threats and continued need for caution.

"You mean with my mother and father?" Kade watched Brooke dance with her father, warmth spreading through him.

"Yeah. Doesn't it seem strange after all this time?"

"A little. In a good way, though. It's obvious they've been in love a long time."

Nesto considered this as he took another swallow of his drink, letting the amber liquid burn a trail down his throat. "I suppose it's pretty hard to get over your first real love."

Kade glanced over at him, surprised at Nesto's words. "Are you talking about my parents, or you and Paige?"

"Hell, man. I'm spouting off, nothing more."

Kade didn't believe a word of it. "If you say so."

Tossing back the last of his drink, Nesto put an arm around Kade's neck, securing him in a headlock. "You're going to be a father. Who'd have ever thought?" Releasing him, he stepped away, his gaze locking on Brooke and the woman standing next to her. "Aw hell."

"What is it? You finally found some hot chick to spend some time with?" Kade's smile faded when his eyes locked on Paige. "Where'd she come from?"

"Damned if I know." He'd built a life without her, done all he could to put her out of his mind, yet there she stood, beautiful and tempting. "She called a few weeks ago, told me Brooke had invited her out. Guess she wanted to warn me."

"Brooke told me to expect her. I didn't know she meant today. Come on. Might as well get this over with." Kade liked Paige. Everyone thought she and Nesto would marry.

"I don't know…"

"Now, Nesto. It's time to man-up."

Paige laughed at Brooke's comment, doing her best not to search the crowd for Nesto. She knew he'd be here. There was no way he'd miss the wedding of his best friend's mother and father. Her hope had been to arrive when Nesto was on one of his many business trips. Instead, Brooke had pleaded for her to be present when she and Kade made their official announcement about being pregnant. Well, she'd come. Now all she wanted was to take her bags and move into the cabin next to Brooke and Kade.

"I'm so happy for you. You're going to make great parents." Paige's heart squeezed. At one time, she'd been able to envision her future with Nesto, surrounded by several children. Instead, she had a choice to make. It had crushed her, but she'd do it again if the circumstances were the same.

"Hey, Paige. When did you get here?"

She turned to see Kade walk up, her breath catching at the sight of Nesto a few feet behind him. Pushing down the ball of dread in her stomach, she forced a smile, doing her best not to meet Nesto's hostile gaze.

"Hi, Kade. I just got in this morning. I couldn't miss my best friend's announcement."

"Well, it's good to have you here." Hugging her, he turned to Nesto. "Of course, you remember this guy."

Sucking in an unsteady breath, she nodded. "Hey, Nesto."

His gaze drilled into hers as he advanced, stopping a foot away, his body vibrating with tension and anger too long ignored. Letting his gaze wander over her, taking in every detail that first attracted him to her, he did his best to push aside the resentment burning inside. Returning to meet her anxious stare, he fisted his hands at his sides.

Ignoring her greeting, he glanced at Kade and nodded, then turned on his heel and walked away.

Join me in the continuation of the MacLarens of Fire Mountain Contemporary series with Foolish Heart, Book Nine

She walked away once. Now she's back. Too bad someone may want her to disappear for good. Start reading **Foolish Heart**!

If you want to keep current on all my preorders, new releases, and other happenings, sign up for my newsletter: https://www.shirleendavies.com/contact-me.html

A Note from Shirleen

Thank you for taking the time to read **'Til the Sun Comes Up!**

If you enjoyed it, please consider telling your friends or posting a short review. Word of mouth is an author's best friend and much appreciated.

I care about quality, so if you find something in error, please contact me via email at shirleen@shirleendavies.com

Books by Shirleen Davies

Contemporary Western Romance Series
MacLarens of Fire Mountain

Second Summer, Book One
Hard Landing, Book Two
One More Day, Book Three
All Your Nights, Book Four
Always Love You, Book Five
Hearts Don't Lie, Book Six
No Getting Over You, Book Seven
'Til the Sun Comes Up, Book Eight
Foolish Heart, Book Nine

Macklins of Whiskey Bend

Thorn, Book One
Del, Book Two
Boone, Book Three

Historical Western Romance Series

Redemption Mountain

Redemption's Edge, Book One
Wildfire Creek, Book Two
Sunrise Ridge, Book Three
Dixie Moon, Book Four
Survivor Pass, Book Five
Promise Trail, Book Six
Deep River, Book Seven

Courage Canyon, Book Eight
Forsaken Falls, Book Nine
Solitude Gorge, Book Ten
Rogue Rapids, Book Eleven
Angel Peak, Book Twelve
Restless Wind, Book Thirteen
Storm Summit, Book Fourteen
Mystery Mesa, Book Fifteen
Thunder Valley, Book Sixteen
A Very Splendor Christmas, Holiday Novella, Book
Seventeen
Paradise Point, Book Eighteen,
Silent Sunset, Book Nineteen
Rocky Basin, Book Twenty, Coming Next in the Series!

MacLarens of Fire Mountain

Tougher than the Rest, Book One
Faster than the Rest, Book Two
Harder than the Rest, Book Three
Stronger than the Rest, Book Four
Deadlier than the Rest, Book Five
Wilder than the Rest, Book Six

MacLarens of Boundary Mountain

Colin's Quest, Book One,
Brodie's Gamble, Book Two
Quinn's Honor, Book Three
Sam's Legacy, Book Four
Heather's Choice, Book Five
Nate's Destiny, Book Six
Blaine's Wager, Book Seven
Fletcher's Pride, Book Eight

Bay's Desire, Book Nine
Cam's Hope, Book Ten

Romantic Suspense

Eternal Brethren, Military Romantic Suspense

Steadfast, Book One
Shattered, Book Two
Haunted, Book Three
Untamed, Book Four
Devoted, Book Five
Faithful, Book Six
Exposed, Book Seven
Undaunted, Book Eight
Resolute, Book Nine
Unspoken, Book Ten
Defiant, Book Eleven, Coming Next in the Series!

Peregrine Bay, Romantic Suspense

Reclaiming Love, Book One
Our Kind of Love, Book Two
Edge of Love, Book Three, Coming Next in the Series!

Find all of my books at:
https://www.shirleendavies.com/books.html

About Shirleen

Shirleen Davies writes romance—historical, contemporary, and romantic suspense. She grew up in Southern California, attended Oregon State University, and has degrees from San Diego State University and the University of Maryland. Her passion is writing emotionally charged stories of flawed people who find redemption through love and acceptance. She now lives with her husband in a beautiful town in northern Arizona.

I love to hear from my readers!

Send me an email: shirleen@shirleendavies.com
Visit my Website: https://www.shirleendavies.com/
Sign up to be notified of New Releases:
https://www.shirleendavies.com/contact/
Follow me on Amazon:
http://www.amazon.com/author/shirleendavies
Follow me on BookBub:
https://www.bookbub.com/authors/shirleen-davies

Other ways to connect with me:

Facebook Author Page:
http://www.facebook.com/shirleendaviesauthor
Twitter: www.twitter.com/shirleendavies
Pinterest: http://pinterest.com/shirleendavies
Instagram: https://www.instagram.com/shirleendavies_author/

www.ingramcontent.com/pod-product-compliance
Lightning Source LLC
Chambersburg PA
CBHW071744190726
48292CB00003B/861